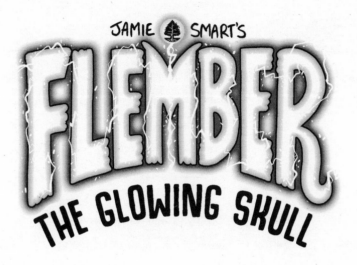

JAMIE SMART'S

FLEMBER

THE GLOWING SKULL

D1513273

www.davidficklingbooks.com

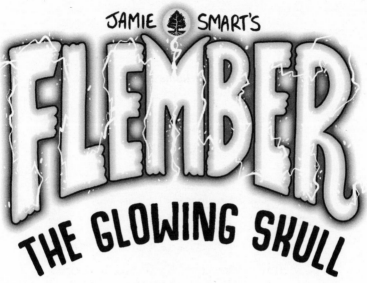

JAMIE SMART'S

FLEMBER

THE GLOWING SKULL

David Fickling Books

31 Beaumont Street
Oxford OX1 2NP, UK

FLEMBER: The Glowing Skull
is a
DAVID FICKLING BOOK

First published in Great Britain in 2021 by
David Fickling Books,
31 Beaumont Street,
Oxford, OX1 2NP

Text and illustrations © Jamie Smart, 2021
Colouring of inside artwork by Emily Kimbell

978-1-78845-150-5

1 3 5 7 9 10 8 6 4 2

Papers used by David Fickling Books are from well-
managed forests and other responsible sources.

MIX
Paper from
responsible sources
FSC® C018072

DAVID FICKLING BOOKS Reg. No. 8340307

A CIP catalogue record for this book is
available from the British Library.

Printed and bound in Great Britain by Clays, Ltd, Elcograf S.p.A

You can't control everything

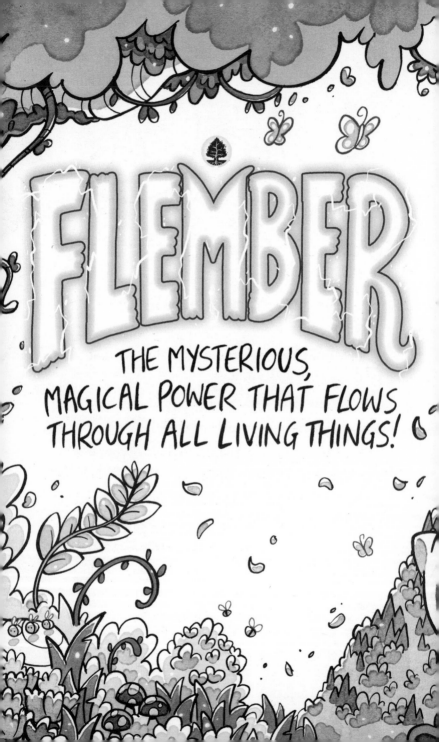

What Happened Before

FLEMBER! The mysterious, magical power that flows through all living things!

Dev P. Everdew is a young inventor whose ideas rarely went to plan. But when he discovered the secret flember book, it threw his whole village into chaos! It showed him how to build Boja – a huge red robot bear, brought to life by the magical power of flember – but in doing so he also accidentally destroyed the Eden Tree, the most beloved tree in his village. Fortunately, the book held one more secret – a map hidden inside its pages. A map that showed all of

Flember Island, including every spot where Dev might find enough flember to bring the Eden Tree back to life.

So Dev and Boja set off to follow the source of all flember – the Flember Stream. Their journey took them through the dark, dangerous forests known as the Wildening, before leading them to a small mining town called Darkwater. Darkwater, however, was a harsh place to live, with very little flember of its own. And the only food that grew there, the explosive hibbicus, gave Boja some rather fiery farts that

ended up destroying most of the town and cutting off access to the Flember Stream!

Only Dev's ingenuity saved the townsfolk, before he and Boja left by tunnel, to try and find some more flember.

Heading for a point on the map marked 'Prosperity' . . .

1
A New Start

The hatch door opened with barely a touch.

Dev pulled himself up and through.

The tunnel had led into a small, dark room. There were no windows here, no furniture. Just a length of railway track leading up and out towards a large metal door, beneath which crept the thinnest crack of daylight.

'GNNNUUUUU!' Boja groaned. He had managed to squeeze his nose, one of his eyeballs, and his right arm out through the hatch, but the rest was proving more difficult. This was, after all, a hole wide enough to fit a mine cart, not a huge robot bear.

'Boja, breathe in.' Dev tugged on a furry red ear. 'Breathe IN!'

Boja did as he was told, gripping onto the tracks and pushing the rest of his head out with a loud POP! Then he sucked his considerable belly in and slowly, slo-w-wly, squeezed the rest of his body through.

He ducked beneath the low ceiling.

Ruffled his furry body back into shape.

'Breakfast?' He beamed hopefully.

It had been a long walk from Darkwater. Countless hours spent trudging through cold, dark tunnels, guided only by the glow of flember flickering out from the tip of Boja's finger. The big hungry bear had consumed a large quantity of flonion soup before they set off, but that had only lasted so long inside his belly. By his last flonion-y

6

burp he was already talking about food again, mainly by listing his favourite biscuits as far as he could count (three biscuits). And then he started asking when he and Dev might have breakfast.

A few minutes later he asked again.

And then again. And again.

And again and again and again.

Now, the mere mention of the word 'breakfast' made Dev's eye twitch. '*Soon.*' He smiled politely. 'Boja, we'll get some food as soon as we can. In fact, there might even be some just outside this door.'

The door, however, looked firmly clenched shut. All manner of elaborate locks covered its surface. Thick white cables ran between them, snaking towards a bulging glass orb in its centre.

Dev ran his fingers around the edge of it. 'All these cogs ready to turn, all these bolts ready to slide,' he whispered. Suddenly he felt an open slot. A thrill ran across his skin. 'So all we need is a KEY!'

He clonked his fist against the side of his helmet. The two cat ears either side of it slid apart. What sputtered out had once been the tools of Dev's Tinkering Helmet – a mesh of lights and lenses to help him invent – but since a fight with his brother Santoro back in Eden, all that now remained was a bundle of broken metal arms. Still, Dev snapped one off, then another, twisting and winding them together until they formed what looked like a key.

A twisted, wonky key.

'It won't be a perfect fit . . .' He held onto the orb with one hand, sliding the key underneath it with the other. 'But it should be just enough . . .'

Click!

'That sounded like a clacklescrew,' he whispered, just as a string of lights flickered along the outer line of cables. They glowed with such a beautiful sparkle that Dev instantly recognized what they were. 'Flemberthysts,' he gasped. 'Boja, there are flemberthyst crystals studded into the cables, and they're filling with—'

'FLEMB-UH!' Boja cheered, raising his fists triumphantly and accidentally punching two dents into the ceiling.

Holding his breath, Dev twisted the key further.

Click!

More flember rushed through the cables, flowing closer towards the orb.

'That's the rufflehinge unlocking.' Dev beamed, barely able to contain himself.

Click!

Click click click!

'Knucklebolts! Farplenuts! Lock-jawed Whistlesprings!'

Suddenly the whole door was shining, a string of lights PLINK-PLINK-PLINK-ing towards the glass orb in its centre until it too was alight.

CONTRAPTION: Flember Door (Dev's best guess)

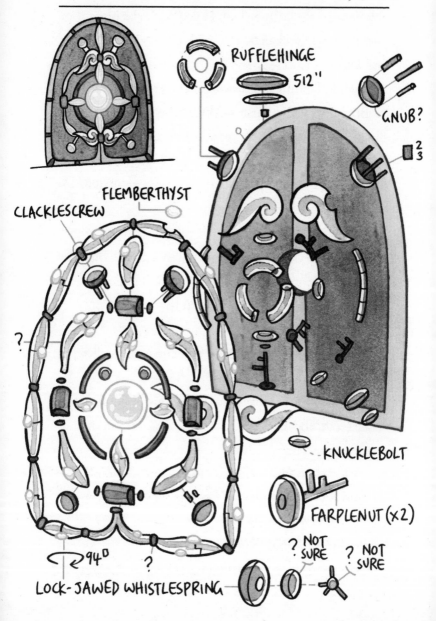

RUFFLEHINGE

512"

GNUB?

2
3

FLEMBERTHYST

CLACKLESCREW

?

KNUCKLEBOLT

FARPLENUT (x2)

? NOT SURE   ? NOT SURE

94°   ?

LOCK-JAWED WHISTLESPRING

Dev pulled his key away just as Boja pushed his size-able face in for a closer look. The door's elaborate arms and hinges unlocked – CLUNK, CLANK, CLUNK – and with a loud creak the door shunted open. Boja fell through it, landing face first onto the ground.

Bright sunlight burst in. Dev held his hand up to shield his eyes. A warm, gentle breeze stroked against his cheek, as if it was washing all memory of the dark tunnels away with it. Slowly, ever so slowly, the landscape around him blinked into view.

And his heart sank.

The ground beneath his boots was barren. Dry. Not a tree or a shrub as far as he could see. No flowers. No grass. Not even a bobbleberry bush.

Just dust. And rock.

'Oh, not again.' He sighed. 'Boja, this place looks as dead as Darkwater!'

Dev slipped his backpack from his shoulders and hauled out the flember book. He flipped through its pages, found chapter three, then carefully placed each page on the ground, one next to the other. He plucked the golden, flember-filled F from the book's cover and placed it down upon them.

Bright, beautiful blue flember sparkled across the pages. It traced along all the invisible lines of flemberthyst dust hidden between the words, spreading out through the whole chapter to reveal a map.

A *glowing* map.

Dev counted the measurements along each line, as he tried to work out where he and Boja might be. 'We've walked far enough,' he muttered. 'We really *should* be in Prosperity.' He looked over his shoulder, to a thick concrete wall behind them. It carved a line between the dead ground and a row of pointed green treetops beyond.

'Over that wall must be the *Wildening*.' Dev nervously ran his hand across the blackened scratches on his arm, shivering at the memory of it. Then he turned back to the map, to the cluster of trees upon the third page, and the oval line keeping them all out. 'The wall marks the very edge of Prosperity. So this must be the place, it *must*.'

'Prsprrty.' Boja lifted himself onto his feet and raised a paw against the sunlight. His large bulging eyes squinted ahead of him, across the ground, towards a glimmer of twinkling, shining lights on the horizon.

'You think that's Prosperity, over there?' Dev asked.

'Breakfast!' Boja agreed.

Dev lifted the F away from the pages. Wisps of flember rolled back as the map disappeared. He then shuffled the book back in order and tucked it inside his backpack.

'Well whatever it is' – Dev nodded – 'it's the next point on our map.'

2
The Racetrack

Shadows started to emerge beneath the shimmering lights. Shadows which became shapes, which became buildings: small, crumbling little houses, each built from stone and wood, their roofs woven from straw. Washing lines hung between them, barrels stacked beside them. Half-loaded carts lay abandoned in the middle of the road.

'Hello?' Dev called out.

'HELLO!' Boja cheerfully replied, lifting one of the straw roofs off its walls and wearing it like a hat.

'Not you,' Dev hushed. He listened out for any other reply, but couldn't hear anyone. 'It seems like everyone left their houses in a hurry.'

Suddenly his foot caught on something in the ground. He stumbled onto his knees. For a second he hoped, perhaps, it might have been a tree root, but on closer inspection it was a cable lined with flemberthysts, just like the ones he'd seen in the metal door.

And it too was glowing.

'It's carrying flember,' he gasped, before noticing more cables half-buried by the dust. Each of them studded with glowing flemberthysts. 'They're *all* carrying flember, and they're coming from . . .'

The wind changed direction. A murmur of noises rode upon it.

Voices.

Lots of voices.

'This way!' Dev yelled, jumping back onto his feet and running between the buildings. Boja followed, squeezing through the cramped alleys, leaping up the huge stone steps, stomping up the steeper ground. Higher and higher they went. The path narrowed. The buildings stacked tighter around them.

The voices grew louder now. Rushing, roaring, breaking into cheers. 'BREAKFAST!' Boja yelled back, assuming everyone cheered for breakfast the same way he did. With the exciting thought of food to power him on he took the lead, bounding up between the buildings, tongue flapping, arms waving, his straw-roof hat tumbling from his head.

17

'They're not . . . *puff* . . . chanting for breakfast!' Dev's legs were aching, his heart pounding. When the path finally ran out he thought he might be able to catch up, but Boja just leapt against a wall and started climbing. Dev clambered after him, pulling himself up from brick to brick, before finally gripping the weathered edges of a gutter and he-e-e-aving himself up.

And then he FLUMP-ed, exhausted, in amongst a crowd of feet.

The people around him must have numbered in their hundreds, thousands even, all of them spread across a seemingly endless row of rooftops. They were dressed in tatty old clothes, torn trousers, split boots. They cheered, and they booed, and they swore like Dev hadn't heard since that time he'd snuck into Eden's hibbicus beer halls.

He crawled between their feet, calling out for Boja as if his voice could ever be heard over the noise.

And then, suddenly, he reached the farthest edge.

And he could see what had been casting such bright lights.

A spire, a magnificent, bulging spire, so tall it almost punctured the clouds. Its glass sides reflected the dazzling sunlight, while a net of pulsing cables threaded across them, each pitted with huge chunks of glowing flember-thyst crystals. They ran from the spire's pointed tip right down to the wide, open concourse, then trailed out across a thick bustle of treetops.

'So *this* must be Prosperity,' Dev gasped. 'And it looks like they've built it right on top of the Flember Stream!'

He cast his eyes down to where the crowd's attention was focused. A racetrack, six lanes, each lit up in bright colours, that ran all the way around the spire in one huge loop.

And in each lane stood a racer.

The first three racers were tall, proud, and clad in a sleek metallic white armour. Lights ran down their arms and legs, lights that blinked on and off as they moved. The next three racers, however, looked quite different. They looked . . . smaller. Their armour was old and battered, as if it had been cobbled together from junk. Rusty exhaust pipes stuck out from their backs. Puffs of dark grey smoke trailed out behind them.

'Brianne's been working day and night on her armour.' A man nudged Dev. He was tall, friendly looking, and smiling proudly through a beard so big it looked like he could hide small animals inside it. 'That's her.' He nodded. 'Fourth lane along. "Rails, I can win this year," she keeps telling me. "I have the best chance out of *anyone.*" Well, I hope she's right. It might finally make things fair around here.'

The racer in the fourth lane looked up at them. Her face was mostly obscured by the huge jaws of her rusty helmet, but Dev could see her bright green eyes. They stared at him with a furious determination.

Dev waved back, an excited grin across his face.

'What's going on here?' he asked Rails. 'Why are they all racing?'

'For a share of Prosperity's flember, of course!' Rails crossed his arms and, as he did, Dev caught sight of a strap clamped around his wrist. It glowed with the light of a flemberthyst crystal. 'How could *anyone* not know about the Pioneer Races?'

'You . . . you're *wearing* a flemberthyst,' Dev stammered. 'Where did you get it from?'

Rails stared down at Dev's wrists in bemusement. 'Question is . . .' he said, 'why ain't *you* wearing a harness?'

'AGAIN!' Boja suddenly called out. Dev turned and saw the bear a little further along the rooftops, surrounded by a flock of rather stunned onlookers. In front of him stood a small boy, his chestnut hair ruffled, his clothes a little shabby. A delighted grin spread between his cheeks. He held a family-sized bag of snacks – salty, crunchy bufflechips, to be precise – as Boja hopped back and forth in front of him, panting like a dog.

Then the boy slowly reached into the bag, pulled out a bufflechip, and flung it into the air as high as he could.

Boja's mouth opened wide. He watched the bufflechip as it arced down towards him, and then . . .

'CHOMP!' Boja chewed. The wide-eyed crowd roared with laughter. 'CHOMP CHOMP CHOMP!'

'Breakfast?' Dev laughed.

'Brckfschtt!' Boja gleefully chomped in reply.

'GOOD PEOPLE OF PROSPERITY!' A loud voice spoke, silencing the crowd. Dev looked around to see where it had come from and spotted a number of huge, floating screens hovering above the racetrack. A woman's face appeared upon them. She was pale but for her

unnaturally rosy red cheeks, whilst her starkly white hair had been bundled into wide loops and held in place by a series of ornate golden pins.

'We are gathered' – she spoke through delicately

23

painted lips – 'for the most important date in our city's calendar. Ladies and gentlemen, boys and girls, welcome to the *Pioneer Races!*'

A loud cheer erupted, as the crowd around Dev jostled and shoved each other with excitement. Through the glass walls of the spire, he could see people excitedly punching the air inside. Their clothes looked a lot smarter. Their hair was trimmed into neater shapes. Their surroundings were a lot more luxurious than the crumbling old rooftop Dev was standing on.

'What's a Pionee—' Dev started, only for an almighty 'SHRIEK!' to drown out his voice. He swung around in time to see a badly aimed bufflechip bouncing off Boja's big black nose, over his head and into the crowd.

'SHRIEK!' Boja went again as he lunged after it, a wild panic in his eyes. Innocent bystanders leapt out of his way. 'Sorry!' he whimpered, accidentally crumpling a few of them. 'SORRY!'

What happened next seemed to occur in slow motion. The bufflechip rolled past Dev's boot, too fast for him to catch it, or even stamp on it, before dropping off the edge of the rooftop. He turned, opening his mouth to warn Boja, but before he could get any of the words out Boja was already bowling past him. Off the roof and into the air, over the racetrack. All six racers stared up in befuddlement at the huge, shrieking shadow sailing over them and then – THUMP! – Boja landed, his huge wobbly bottom slamming down into the sixth lane, clipping the poor racer who was already standing there and sending them tumbling over the edge of the track.

Down the racer fell, in amongst the treetops, before disappearing from sight altogether.

The crowd held its breath.

'DOLLOP?' Rails yelled out.

'I'm OK!' a beleaguered voice finally wailed, to which the crowd sighed with relief.

Boja, meanwhile, stood in a butt-crater of his own making, shaking his head as if it might stop his eyes rolling around in their sockets. 'BUFFLECHIP,' he moaned. 'BUFFLECHIIIIIP!'

'Boja, get back up here,' Dev hissed. 'They'll think you're in the race!'

'Maybe . . . he could be!' Rails exclaimed. 'We're one racer down now, and your bear's already taken her place! He looks fast. Or at least, he looks strong. Well . . . *bulky*. He looks bulky. That might give us an advantage.'

Suddenly Dev became very aware that the crowd had hushed. They all stared at him expectantly.

'Please?' Rails asked. 'We could use all the help we can get.'

3
The First Race

'BUFFLECHIP!' Boja gasped, spying his salty prize wedged into a crevice between the armoured neck slats of Ralto, the largest racer. Boja crept closer, as discreetly as a huge clumsy bear can. Then he reached out his arm, and opened his finger and thumb apart as if he were about to steal the most precious jewel imaginable.

'Bu-u-u-u-fflechip . . .' he whined.

'Boja!' Dev called out. He carefully slid himself over the edge of the rooftops and then down, stepping cautiously onto the racetrack. 'Boja, they want you to race for them! And they're one racer down now, so I guess we *should* help.'

Brianne leant back from the other racers to get a good look at Boja. 'Just as long as he doesn't butt-nudge *me* over the edge too,' she grumbled.

'YOU ALL KNOW THE RULES!' the white-haired lady on the screens declared, making Dev jump in surprise. 'Racers must complete a full lap of the race-track, round Prosperity's boundary, and all the way back to the First Pioneer.'

Dev turned. There, behind all the racers, towered a rather large statue. He'd barely noticed it before, what with so many sights to take in and chasing after Boja. Now, however, he saw it in detail.

Rolls of white hair. Sharp cheekbones. Thin, painted lips.

A pair of curious stone compasses held between its hands.

'I do, of course, mean the statue of ME,' the lady announced, a wry smile fluttering between her cheeks. 'As First Pioneer I, Grace Neverwhere, am the architect of everything you see around you. I designed Prosperity itself. I had it built as a home for us all. And now our brightest and best will compete to honour my very name.'

The crowd inside the Spire cheered enthusiastically.

'Just run around the track with the rest of them,' Dev whispered, tugging on Boja's butt fur to get his attention. 'I'll be waiting here for you at the end of the race.'

Boja was not listening, however. He was still transfixed by the bufflechip.

'Boja!' Dev insisted, clambering up Boja's back until he was whispering right into his fluffy red ear. 'If we win the race, maybe they'll take us to the Flember Stream. Then we can go home and . . .'

His voice tailed off. He too had become distracted, not by a bufflechip but by the images of Grace upon the screens. For she now held an object proudly between her hands. It was bulky, round. It was glowing.

And it stared back at Dev through two hollow eye sockets.

A cold shiver rattled down through his spine.

'Is that . . .' he gasped. 'Is that a human *skull*?'

'Oh, you have no *idea*.' Brianne smirked.

'Complete the race, climb the statue and claim the COMPASS!' Grace shouted, as the skull glowed even brighter in her hands. 'AND MAY THE BEST RACER WIN!'

A ridiculously loud HON-N-N-N-NKKKK echoed across Prosperity. The crowd erupted into a deafening cheer. 'No one stands a chance against ME,' Esco, the first racer, snarled. His armour lit up in a blaze of blue lights and then suddenly he was gone, surging ahead at an extraordinary speed, his cape billowing out behind him. The second racer, Sienna, did the same, gliding gracefully along the racetrack as she sped into the distance.

Brianne, in the fourth lane, gave chase. She clanked and wheezed as she ran, but what her armour lacked in finesse, she more than made up for in determination. Pipo, the smallest racer, ran in the lane beside her, only to be closely pursued by Ralto. Huge, hulking Ralto. He roared as he stomped between the lanes, one heavy foot after the other, lights flickering wildly across his chest.

Boja was left standing, arm outstretched, pinching at the air. 'Bufflechip?'

Dev winced, clutching a little tighter onto Boja's ears. 'Can I just get down fir—'

'BUFFLECHIP!' Boja boomed, raising his arms in the air and balling his paws into fists. Then with an excited little squeak, he too was part of the race, his eyes bulging wide, his tongue flapping behind him. Dev found himself clinging on for dear life. Terrified, he squeezed his eyes shut as the cheers of the crowd echoed between his ears.

By the time Dev had opened his eyes again Boja was already halfway around the track, running beneath the shadows of the spire itself. While the other racers were still some distance ahead of them – Esco first, then Sienna, with Brianne and Pipo trailing behind – Boja's hunger had driven him within a tigglesnatch's whisker of his own prize: Ralto, or rather, the bufflechip wedged into his armour. 'Bu-u-u-ufflechip,' Boja puffed, arms outstretched, fingers desperately waggling out in front of him.

Ralto caught sight of the big, hungry bear, and he snarled. The lights across his armour blazed even brighter and then suddenly he was gone, faster than before, his huge metal feet clanging loudly towards Pipo. Pipo yelped in alarm only for Ralto to leap upon him, clamping one of his huge armoured claws around Pipo's waist and lifting the tiny racer off the track. 'You might as well just give up NOW!' Ralto boomed, flinging Pipo over his shoulder like a water balloon. Boja swerved. Dev ducked. Pipo CLANG-CLANG-CLANG-ed along behind them.

'That . . . that *must* be cheating!' Dev cried.

Boja growled, scrunching his face up in fury. Flember crackled across his fur, sparkling out from his nostrils, powering him on faster and faster.

And closer to Ralto.

'BUFFLECHIP!' he cheered, reaching out, only for Ralto to swing back and clamp his claw down hard around the bear's arm. Flember burst out from beneath Boja's fur, spinning around his body in random bursts.

'BOJA!' Dev cried, clinging on tight as Boja buckled to his knees and Ralto dragged him along the racetrack like a huge floppy doll. Boja roared in pain, and he whimpered, and he belched out huge plumes of sparkling flember. But he couldn't find his feet, couldn't work his way loose of the claw.

'Maybe I can undo it!' Dev heaved himself across Boja's body, pulling himself up, over the bear's face, along his outstretched arm. Then he pulled the makeshift key from his pocket, leant in through the sparkling bursts of flember and wedged it in between the hinges of Ralto's claw. 'It can't be that complicated,' he muttered. 'A few ruffleclanks, maybe a lock-ping bolt, I've unlocked far worse.'

'HOI!' Ralto swung his other claw to bat Dev away, but Dev was quick to duck. It was enough, however, to throw Ralto completely off balance, his huge metal feet falling over each other and the huffing, puffing racer came crashing face first onto the racetrack, rolling with Boja – and Dev – on top of him.

With all three of them crumpled in a heap, Boja's arm still clamped inside Ralto's claw, the big red bear reached his other arm out towards the only thing in the world that could lessen the pain.

'Bufflechip . . .' he whimpered.

'The race . . . isn't . . . over . . . yet,' Ralto moaned, just as the lights on his armour started to flash again. Small rockets around his feet started to ignite. FOOM! FOOM! FOOM!

'Oh, what now?' Dev winced, just as Ralto's whole body started sliding forwards like a train, dragging them both along with him. Within seconds they were powering forwards at a speed that defied the sheer weight Ralto was carrying. Along the final stretch they sped, weaving chaotically across the lanes, until Dev could see Brianne only a short distance ahead, and then – BUMP! – she, too, was lifted up, and rolled onto Ralto's back beside him. Dev tried to help her upright but then – BUMP! Sienna. BUMP! Esco. All of them screaming furiously as they rocketed along the final stretch towards the statue.

Unable to stop.

Unable, even, to slow down.

That is until Ralto's rockets suddenly spluttered, and then exploded, just a short distance away from the statue. The whole train skidded to a halt in a tangled heap of arms, legs and smoke.

A deafening hush fell across the crowds.

Brianne was first to crawl out from the smoke. Her armour was thoroughly battered. Bits of it were still on fire.

She slowly, and in some discomfort, dragged herself towards the statue.

And then a bufflechip rolled out alongside her.

She looked down at it, bewildered.

Boja suddenly burst out from the smoke, the claw from Ralto's armour still firmly clamped around his arm (albeit with no Ralto attached to the other end). He threw himself past Brianne, his puckering lips poking out as far as they could reach as he FLUMP-ed his face down upon the bufflechip like a wilderhog pouncing upon its prey.

CHOMP!

He lay, chewing and moaning with delight.

Seeing her chance, Brianne heaved herself upright and then started climbing up, over Boja's dusty bottom, his back, his head, before hauling herself up the statue itself. Hovering between Grace's stone hands she found the prize they had all been racing for.

The *stone compass*.

She grabbed it, and held it high above her head.

HO-O-O-ONKKKKKK! A second klaxon sounded. The crowd went wild. A confetti of bufflechips rained down from the sky.

'We have a WINNER!' The white-haired lady appeared across the screens once again. Triumphant images of a happy, chewing bear flashed alongside her, before scanning up to the exhausted-looking girl still clinging to the statue. 'Good people of Prosperity, for the first time in our history, a Pioneer Race has been claimed by a LESSER!'

'A what?' Dev coughed and spluttered his way out from the smoke, glancing back at all the battered and exhausted racers still spread across the racetrack, before gazing up towards the screens.

Where the white-haired lady was smiling politely.

The glowing skull still clutched between her hands.

'This place is so *WEIRD*,' Dev puffed.

4

The Moving City

'Boja, are you OK?' Dev winced, skidding down beside Boja, gripping onto Ralto's huge metal claw and trying to heave it apart.

Boja's lips sucked up a few stray bufflechip crumbs from the racetrack. Then he lifted his face up towards Dev, blinked the one eye that was still open, and grinned a rather satisfied grin.

'Buf-f-fflechips.'

'That BEAR!' a voice cried from behind them. It was the sixth racer, Dollop, the one Boja had accidentally butt-nudged off the racetrack. She had climbed back up from the treetops.

'I'm really sorry,' Dev started. 'Boja didn't mean to—'

'THAT BEAR helped us WIN!' Dollop cried in delight, hobbling towards Boja and enthusiastically patting his bottom like a drum. 'Thanks to you two, we've FINALLY won a Pioneer Race!'

Brianne slid down from the statue, unscrewed her helmet, and released a plait of bright orange hair down alongside her oil-smeared face. 'We worked well as a team.' She smiled, waving to Pipo as he limped along the track. 'All of us. We won this race together.'

She admired the stone compass in her hand. 'Maybe . . .' Her pale green eyes started to glisten. 'Maybe we finally have a chance to change things around here.'

Suddenly an almighty clanking noise rose around them. The rooftops upon which the crowds had been standing started to rattle, the old stone buildings beneath them started to shake. Great plumes of dust spilled out across the racetrack. And then, to Dev's amazement, the buildings started to . . . *sink*.

'It's an EARTHQUAKE!' Dev shouted, gripping

tightly onto Boja's fur.

'It's no such thing,' Brianne chuckled, stepping onto a rooftop as it passed below her feet. 'The ground around Prosperity lifts everyone up to watch the race. Then it sinks back down once the race is over.'

Dev heard the words, but still he couldn't quite piece them together. 'The ground . . . lifts UP? How does the ground lift UP?'

'Brianne, you won!' Rails cried, wrapping a proud arm around Brianne's shoulders as the rooftop lowered him down. 'You actually did it!'

'I told you.' Dev saw Brianne beam with delight as the two of them disappeared from view. 'I *knew* we had a chance this year.'

A groan came from behind the statue. The three other racers on the track, the ones in the sleek, flashy armour, were finally stirring. Limb by limb they started untangling themselves from each other.

Sienna staggered to her feet. She stared at Dev with a chilling glare.

'I . . . I think maybe we should get off the racetrack,' Dev whispered nervously, sliding his fingers into Boja's paw.

Boja, however, didn't grip back. His paw was limp, flopping around like a wet sock, the fur ruffled, the claw still clamped around the twisted metal bones of his arm. Boja's teeth bit down into his bottom lip. 'Hurts,' he whimpered.

'It must do.' Dev sympathized, as he looked over the edge of the racetrack and then down, across the sinking rooftops. 'So, come on, let's get you fixed up.'

Climbing up through a mound of buildings was one thing, but climbing back down, while they were sinking, was something else entirely. The ground lowered itself in sections, CLUNK-ing loudly back into place. Steps flattened down into paths. Whole buildings rattled back beside each other. And it was only now, in amongst it all, that Dev noticed the mechanical parts attached to everything. Cogs turned, pistons fired, hinges creaked and flexed. And there were cables everywhere, like the ones buried in the ground, like the ones stretched around the spire: thick, white cables studded with an endless trail of flemberthyst crystals.

Each of them glowing with flember.

'I guess this is where all of Darkwater's flemberthysts ended up,' Dev puffed excitedly, pulling Boja through an alleyway only moments before the buildings either side of them slid back together. 'It feels like being inside a huge *machine*! A whole city moving around us, all of it controlled by the flemberthyst cables!'

He paused for a moment. 'But who's controlling the *cables*?'

The local residents had clearly seen their city move like this countless times before, because they were too busy celebrating Brianne's win to pay it much attention. They laughed, and sang, riding upon the moving buildings without a care in the world. They only stopped when they caught sight of Boja, the huge furry, sparkling, whimpering, half-blinking bear limping through their streets.

Then they'd all start to cheer.

Dev smiled politely, pulling Boja on as the last few houses CLUNK-CLONK-CLANK-ed into place around them. The mound they had climbed towards the centre of Prosperity was now flat, a network of streets level with the barren ground beyond. They all led towards a tall, round building at the end of the road, as it revolved with a great grinding of gears.

Rails stood in its open doorway.

'Here they are!' Rails cheerfully raised an eyebrow. 'The boy and his big, brilliant bear!'

'Boja needs help,' Dev said, lifting Boja's floppy arm. 'I can't get the claw off, and I don't have any tools to do it. I thought, well . . . I thought if Brianne built her own armour, then maybe she'd have some tools I could borrow?'

'Tools?' Rails squinted curiously at Boja. Boja swayed

on his feet, then belched out a little puff of sparkles. 'What *kind* of tools?'

'A Clickwidget might do it?' Dev suggested hopefully.

Brianne peeked her head out from behind Rails. 'Are you a mechanic too?' she asked.

'I'm an *inventor*.' Dev smiled nervously. 'I, well . . . I invented Boja.'

Rails widened his eyes. '*You* invented *this*?' He looked Boja up and down. 'So what is he, some kind of mechanoid frame? Basic circuit-board controls? Couple of bulgy eyes to amuse the kids?'

'He . . . he's more than that. He's *alive*!'

Rails cautiously extended a gloved finger, and slowly, very slowly, poked it into Boja's soft, furry belly.

A muffled FRRP guffed out from between Boja's buttocks.

'Ahhhhh!' A wide smile crumpled Rails's face into wrinkles. 'You nearly had me! He's alive. ALIVE! AS IF! Hey, Brianne, you see this? Kid here's got some rather clever robot-building skills. Made it fart, of all things!'

'Bring Boja inside.' Brianne beckoned. 'As long as he stays away from the fire, he can fart all he wants.'

CLICKWIDGET

5
The Foundry

As Dev stepped in through the doorway of the Foundry, a thick smell hit his nose. It was the smell of burning, of grease, oil and dirt. He breathed deeply. A smile spread across his lips. This place reminded him of Bastor's forge back in Eden. His ears filled with an orchestra of familiar noises. Clanking, wrenching and crumpling. The thick bubbling of molten metal. The loud crackle of a huge fire in the middle of it all. He watched as a trail of grey smoke sailed up between the rafters, past the bits and pieces of armour hanging from their chains, up through what remained of the collapsed floors, the missing roof and out into the midday sky.

'Clickwidget.' Brianne leant out from behind the Foundry's heaped pile of ovens and slid a Clickwidget across the floor.

'Th . . . thank you.' Dev picked it up. He reached through the doorway, grabbed Boja's other paw and helped the rather sorrowful-looking bear sque-e-e-eeze inside. Then he positioned him in front of the flickering fire.

'Boja, I need you to hold very still.'

'Oh-kay.' Boja smiled nervously.

Dev grabbed one of the chains hanging from the wall, tied it around the claw and heaved Boja's whole arm up to shoulder level. Then he dragged a stepladder across the room and climbed to its height.

'This might hurt a little.'

'Oh-kay.'

'OK.' Dev tenderly patted Boja's arm. Then he wedged the Clickwidget inside the claw, and he twisted it.

'YO-W-W-W-W!' Boja howled. His flember crackled out across his fur.

'Just a little tighter . . .'

Boja howled louder.

His flember burned brighter.

And lo-o-o-o-ouder.

And BRIGHTER.

CLUNK! The claw unlocked.

CLANK! It hit the ground.

'AWOOOOOOWL!' Boja shrieked. His flember blazed out in a huge arc of sparkling blue light, so bright Dev could barely see. Then, gradually, it ebbed back down beneath Boja's fur, as Dev tenderly released his big red floppy arm from the chains.

It flomped down by his side. Withered. Crumpled. Strangely lumpy in places.

'Your arm's *really* broken,' Dev gasped, clambering back down the ladder. 'Oh, Boja, it must be so *painful*!'

Tears wobbled in the corner of Boja's big bulging eyes.

'Is OK,' he whimpered.

'What just HAPPENED?' Rails blinked, half-stunned, half-amazed. 'I can't say I've ever seen a machine feel *pain* before!'

Brianne flanked Boja from the other side. 'This isn't just a machine,' she whispered. 'Just look at all the *flember* inside it!'

'I told you, he . . . he's alive,' Dev insisted. 'Boja's my friend.'

Brianne climbed on top of a smelting pot until she was level with Boja's big shiny nose, and then she

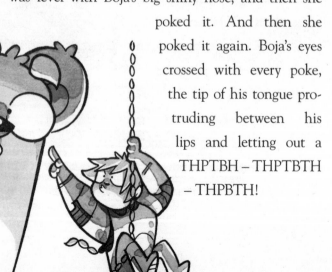

poked it. And then she poked it again. Boja's eyes crossed with every poke, the tip of his tongue protruding between his lips and letting out a THPTBH – THPTBTH – THPBTH!

'Where'd you even find enough flember to get him moving?' She grinned. Then, suddenly, her face fell. 'Hang on . . . did the Primes build this thing? Are you both *Prime*?'

'I . . . I don't know what Prime means,' Dev stuttered.

Brianne jumped down. 'None of us have that kind of technology out here,' she said, edging cautiously away. 'And we certainly don't have enough spare flember to run it.'

'They're not even wearing flember harnesses on their wrists,' Rails laughed. 'I doubt very much they've been anywhere near the Primes.' Rails held out a lump of crumbly, grey cake up towards Boja's mouth. Boja nibbled delicately at it. Then, without warning, Boja's lips slurped over Rails' hand, and with a loud gulp the entire cake was gone.

'I'm sorry, he's always hungry,' Dev explained.

Rails flicked the drool from his fingers. 'Well, it was

only gritcake, hardly a decent meal. But the bear helped us win the first race, so *wherever* he came from he deserves to share in what little we have.'

Brianne muttered to herself, reached into a pocket and pulled out her own carefully wrapped slice of gritcake. 'You *both* helped,' she said, handing the cake to Dev. 'So I guess you can't be all that bad.'

Dev smiled. His belly rumbled. And even though gritcake very much tasted like its name suggested, he bit into it with an immense satisfaction.

'I'm sorry,' he chomped through another mouthful. 'I don't mean to be rude, and I have *so* many questions, but I still need to fix Boja's arm. If I could just borrow a few more tools – a Winchdriver, an Optylopop, maybe a Cogglesnotch . . .'

Brianne and Rails both stared at him blankly.

'A Root-pinioned Fisplestaw?' Dev asked.

'We don't have a whole lot here.' Brianne shrugged. 'They might have tools like that inside the Spire, but . . .'

'Then we'll go to the Spire!' Dev gulped down his last lump of gritcake, then gently gripped Boja's floppy fingers. 'And I'll fix Boja right back to how he was!'

6
The Rolla-Bolla Sewer Ball

'Thank you for the Clickwidget,' Dev called behind him, as he led Boja into the street and through the gaggle of people who had gathered to try to get a glimpse of the bear. 'Me and Boja have to find the Flember Stream if we're ever going to get back home, but to do that, first I have to fix his arm.

'FLOPPY ARM!' Boja smiled, stumbling along behind, lifting his floppy arm to wave at the curious bystanders.

'Dev, you can't just walk into the Spire,' Brianne puffed as she ran after him. 'They don't want people like us in there.'

'But Boja needs help,' Dev said.

'That . . . that's not a good enough reason.'

Dev turned to Boja. Boja whimpered meekly, sniffing back tears.

'Yes it *is*,' Dev insisted.

Rails pushed his way through the crowd. 'Come back to the Foundry, Dev. Maybe we can work out another way to fix your bear.' His voice sounded a little more nervous than usual.

'I don't understand,' Dev cried. 'Why are you all so afraid of going into the Spire?'

A strange noise filled his ears. A slick, slithering noise. It made him feel clammy, uneasy, as if something rather nasty was waiting for them around the next corner. He walked slowly on, turning out from the alleyway and onto a wider street.

He could see movement up ahead.

Rolling, undulating movement.

'The cables!' he gasped.

They squirmed and writhed, flember ebbing between

their brightly glowing flemberthysts, each crystal blinking on and off in a strange, hypnotic pattern.

'Snakes.' Boja gazed, transfixed.

'Not snakes,' Dev replied.

'The boundary keeps us out,' Brianne sighed.

'Where . . . where did all these cables come from?'

'Oh, they've always been here.' Rails added. 'The outskirts hide the boundary when the ground lifts up to watch the race, but it's always here. Always keeping us out.'

Dev edged closer to the boundary, cautiously placing his hand upon one of the cables. He could feel the gentle hum of flember inside it. Could see the fine hairs on his arm prickling up on end.

'But you've no trees out here, no grass, no flowers, all because the city's flember is running through these cables.'

'That's why we race.' Brianne lay a gentle hand on his shoulder. 'If we win, we get to share in Prosperity's flember.'

Dev lifted his eyes to the boundary's very heights, way, way up towards the sky.

'Well, right now me and Boja need to get through, and it's too tall to climb,' he mused, before staring down at his feet. 'So maybe, instead, we could go *under* it!'

He pointed to a manhole cover in the ground. It appeared to be bolted and locked into place, but Dev spied a slot in its centre. A slot just big enough to fit his makeshift key.

He knelt down, pulled the key from his pocket and slid it inside.

CLI-I-I-I-ICK!

CLUNK!

With a proud grin Dev heaved the cover open.

'Oh he's a clever one.' Rails nudged Brianne.

The crowd, too, gasped in admiration, then retched, as a smell of rotten eggs and filth wafted out from inside the hole. 'I – hurgh – crawled around the sewers loads back home in Eden,' Dev announced, perhaps a little too cheerfully. 'Like that time I was looking for – hurgh – subterranean Dingleberry mushrooms! Or the time I hid from my big brother, Santoro, because I got – hurghhhh – hufflepig juice on his new tunic!'

He looked down into the swirling, bubbling darkness, and his enthusiasm started to wither.

'Although this . . . uh, this looks a little deeper than – hurgh – Eden's sewers.'

As soon as the smell hit Boja's nostrils his whole body started to heave, like a cat trying to cough up a huge fur ball. 'Not nice,' he retched, pushing his nose up between his flickering eyelids. 'IT'S NOT NICE!'

'If you really, really want to get inside – hurgh – the Spire,' Brianne winced, 'your best chance would be when all these buildings lift up again. It'll happen in a few hours. If you can just – hurgh – wait.'

'I can't – hurgh – wait.' Dev pulled his scarf up over his nose. 'I have a Boja to fix!' He slipped the backpack from his shoulders. Its front buckle was broken, slammed too hard when Dev was trying to get away from Priest – the flember-thief he had faced in Darkwater – but the inflatable airbag sewn into its lining was still intact.

And it was exactly what he needed.

'Boja, I need you to blow into this,' he said, ripping the airbag out and holding it up like a big deflated balloon.

'OK!' Boja cheered, without questioning it. He inhaled with an enormously loud HU-U-U-U-U-UPPP, put the opening of the airbag to his lips, and blew with all his might.

SQU-U-U-U-UEAK! The airbag inflated far beyond its usual size, bulging out in front of everyone like a big wobbling moon. The bigger it got, the thinner its skin stretched, turning it almost transparent. Dev hopped and jumped around it. 'Little bit more!' he yelled, watching Boja's eyes bulge as his cheeks squished up around them. 'Little bit more . . . aaaaand . . . STOP!'

Boja gasped, his chest expanding out as he breathed back in. HU-U-U-U-U-U-U-UPPP! Dev quickly pinched the opening, then lifted the huge balloon above his head and slowly sque-e-e-ezed it down over himself.

'Boja!' his voice echoed from inside. 'Boja, come in!'

Boja had only just caught his breath again, but whatever Dev was doing it looked fun. With quite some considerable effort he squeezed his whole body inside the balloon, as Dev tied its nozzle into a knot.

'This is how we get through the sewers,' Dev proudly announced, as he and Boja wobbled around inside. 'I'll call it a . . . Rolla-Bolla Sewer Ball!'

Brianne, and the rest of the crowd, all stared back at him.

'Look, I'll show you!' Dev cheered, running on the spot. The balloon didn't move, at least, not until Boja joined in and propelled them both forwards. The speed of it made Dev lose his footing, and suddenly he was

INVENTION 507: The Rolla-Bolla Sewer Ball

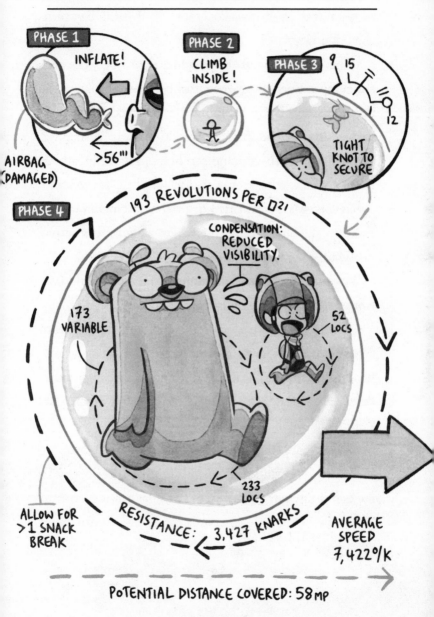

PHASE 1

INFLATE!

AIRBAG (DAMAGED)

>56"'

PHASE 2

CLIMB INSIDE!

PHASE 3

9 15

12

TIGHT KNOT TO SECURE

PHASE 4

193 REVOLUTIONS PER □²¹

CONDENSATION: REDUCED VISIBILITY.

173 VARIABLE

52 LOCS

233 LOCS

ALLOW FOR >1 SNACK BREAK

RESISTANCE: 3,427 KNARKS

AVERAGE SPEED 7,422°/K

POTENTIAL DISTANCE COVERED: 58 MP

being spun around like a biddlebug in a hurricane. 'O-o-o-other way!' he managed to shout. 'B-B-Boja! T-t-t-turn the other way!'

Boja, giggling wildly as he rolled a path between the shrieking onlookers, steered the balloon back towards the boundary. Upon reaching the manhole it stopped, wedged inside the gap, before slo-w-w-w-wly slipping through and then popping out below, splashing into a river of stinky, putrid sewer sludge.

Dev, upside down, gazed in morbid fascination at all the filth slopping around them. 'I'm actually kinda surprised this one works.' He chuckled.

'Are you sure about this plan?' Brianne called down from the bright circle of daylight above them.

'Absolutely positive,' Dev insisted, finding his feet. 'We've come too far to give up now! Me and Boja will head to the Spire, I'll fix Boja, then we'll borrow some flember, and we'll take it home for the Eden Tree! And everything will be fine again!'

'Home!' Boja murmured wistfully.

'Home.' Dev smiled. And with that he and Boja were gone, rolling away into the darkness.

7

An Extraordinary World

Dev and Boja rolled the Rolla-Bolla Sewer Ball across all manner of stinking, bubbling filth until they came upon a ladder clamped to the wall. It led up towards another manhole in the ceiling. 'We climbed in just before the boundary.' Dev grinned, making sure the knot of the ball was facing upwards as he carefully unpicked it. 'So *this* manhole must come out on the other side of it.'

He gripped onto the rungs of the ladder and sque-e-e-eaked himself out of the Rolla-Bolla. Then he climbed up, to the very top, slipping his key into the underside of the manhole cover before cautiously heaving it aside. A beam of warm sunlight shone through, drawing him up the last few rungs and out onto the surface.

Here the ground was quite different. It wasn't squelchy like the sewer, nor dry and dusty like the outskirts. What Dev felt beneath his hands was soft. It was damp.

It was *grass*.

A scent of flowers filled his nose.

A gentle rustle of tree leaves sounded in his ears.

A grunting sounded from the sewers.

'Boja!' Dev yelped. 'Are you OK?'

'Stinky,' Boja grumped, sque-e-e-ezing through the hole in the ground. Dev took the floppy, deflated Sewer Ball from around Boja's ankle and wiped it against the grass. Boja readjusted himself. He sniffed his fur, recoiled dramatically at the smell, shook like a wet dog, then blinked out across their surroundings.

'Pretty-y-y-y.' He smiled.

'It sure is,' Dev agreed.

They stood in what appeared to be woodlands. Great bollup trees towered high above them, each peppered by clouds of billowing neppledrops, fipplesprouts and, around their thick trunks, pink-blotted tulips. Dev plucked a bobonut from one of the leaning fruit willows, chomping down in delight as lumpy green juice dripped from his chin. He stepped down the rocky bank towards a river, scooping handfuls of clear, sparkling water from the ponds and drinking thirstily until his stomach was full.

'DELISCHUS!' Boja peeped from the other bank. He was chewing merrily through something he'd plucked out of the ground, something Dev assumed at first to be

a fruit. Then he realized it was something much, much worse.

It was the top half of a cactus.

A spiky, sharp-needled cactus.

Boja's expression changed mid-chew.

His smile slowly crumpled up into a pained squint.

'OW-W-W-W!' the huge bear whimpered, poking out a huge rubbery tongue embedded with cactus spikes. 'OW OW OW! IBTH HURBTH!'

Dev splashed through the river, hopping around the bear and pulling the spikes out. 'Boja, you can't eat cactus!' he cried. 'Why would you ever even think you *could*?'

'IBTH THARP ON MYPTH THONGUE!' Boja yelped, flailing around before losing his footing completely and tumbling down a bank of trees. Dev ran after him, skidding back out into the sunlight just in time to see the huge bear rolling across a neatly manicured lawn, between perfectly trimmed hedgerows, and then SPLASH!

Boja landed in a pond, spitting out the last of the cactus spines.

Dev waded into the water and pulled the lily pads from Boja's head, only to stop, stunned, as he saw the extraordinary sight rising above them. The *Spire*. This

close up he could see it was held up on three towering columns of stone, with an exceptionally bright light travelling up from the ground beneath it. It shimmered through a thick, transparent pipe, between the columns, and up into the Spire itself.

A light that pulsed like a heartbeat.

'The Flember Stream!' Dev climbed out of the pond, then stepped nervously between the flickering shadows. His legs quivered. His heart pounded. 'They're *pulling* it out from the ground!'

He held a trembling hand out towards the light, only for a rather soggy Boja to rush past him, joyfully slamming himself against the pipe. His one working arm wrapped around it as if he was hugging an old friend.

'THFLEM-BTHHH!' he squealed, closing his eyes in utter joy.

'We've done it,' Dev gazed in amazement. 'Boja, we've found the Flember Stream! Once we get some tools to fix you, well . . . we can take some of this flember *home*!'

Two doors suddenly opened at the front of the pipe. A transparent glass elevator hung inside, holding what appeared to be a small, hovering bin.

'BEEP! RULE 001! All citizens must have their flember registered!' it announced in a tinny, metallic voice.

'How . . . how did you know we were here?' Dev cried in

66

alarm. Then he tilted his head in curiosity. 'Wait . . . are
you a *robot*?' He edged a little closer. A wide grin spreading across his face. 'Are there *robots* inside Prosperity?'

The face on the robot's screen glitched into a frown.
'I am service droid to the First Pioneer. You may address
me as PLOPS.'

'PLOPSTH!' Boja snorted a big bubble of snot from
his left nostril, before lifting a finger and poking it back
in. 'PLOPFTHS PLOMPSCH PLOPSFCTHS!'

'They called you . . . Plops?' Dev stifled a laugh.

'Programmed Leader Of Prime Service,' it declared.
'PLOPS.'

Dev thought for a moment. 'Well, if the Spire has
the tools to build their own robots, then they *must* have
what we would need to fix your arm, Boja! Lead the way,
Plops!'

He stepped inside the elevator, alongside Plops, then gestured for Boja to join them. Boja squeaked with excitement, squeezing himself in, being careful not to bump his sore, floppy arm.

'Robots,' Dev smiled as the glass elevator silently lifted up, carried upon bright, sparkling swirls of flember. 'There are robots here. And here *we* are, actually *inside* the Flember Stream.' He clutched Boja's floppy fingers, and he squeezed them gently.

'I take it back. This place isn't weird at all. Prosperity's INCREDIBLE!'

8
Procedure

The gardens slid away from view as the elevator rose through the basement levels of the Spire. A complex landscape of machinery surrounded them. Pulleys, pumps, pistons and proppleblops, all turning and spinning and heaving against each other. Cables trailed through, around and between them, each bulging with the almost blinding glow of flember.

'BEEP! BEEP! RULE 753!' Plops suddenly barked. 'Unregistered citizens must *not* lick the elevator!'

Boja sheepishly pulled his tongue away from the glass. 'Soh-ree,' he mumbled.

'We'll find a better way for you to borrow some flember.' Dev chuckled. 'I don't think they'll let you lick it through the glass.'

The elevator came to a stop at what was called the ground level. Its doors opened with a gentle PSCHHH. Boja squeezed out first, then Dev, stepping onto a wide glass floor, all manner of machinery churning and glowing brightly beneath their feet. Dev looked up, past the decorative palm trees, up to where the inside of the Spire opened into a broad, open atrium, with balcony upon balcony rising to the uppermost heights. And there, right at the very top of it, a huge swirling mass of cables. They slithered and twisted around each other, crackling with a bright blue light as if it was lightning rolling across thunderclouds.

He stared at it in utter, utter fascination. 'What is tha-a-a-t?' He gasped.

'The fifty-first level is referred to as The Storm, and unfortunately it is out of bounds for all citizens!' A cheerful robotic voice announced. Two droids poked their heads out from behind a desk, friendly faces blinking onto their screens.

'You are, however, allowed to explore all levels

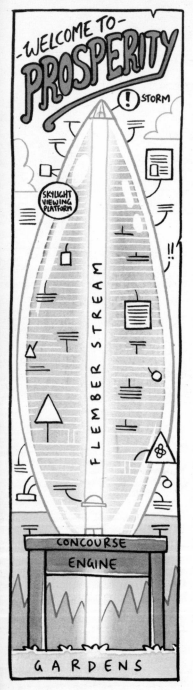

between one and fifty, depending on your permissions!' the other droid added.

'All Prime are welcome to make use of our extensive facilities.' One of the droids whizzed out from behind the desk. Its side panel opened, and a long metal arm extended out, handing Dev a carefully folded piece of paper. 'We would encourage you to relax in the Flember Baths, take a walk in the Lysium Fields, or enjoy the chef droid's Twisted Melon Smoothie in the Skylight Bar.'

'Smooooothie.' Boja drooled.

Dev unfolded the paper, then again, then again, until he was holding an enormous map of the Spire. He ran his finger down all the weird and wonderful levels before finally finding the one he wanted.

'Development Rooms, level four,' he said. 'Now *that* sounds like a good place to find some tools.'

'BEEP! NOT YET REGISTERED.' Plops clonked against Dev's leg. 'Unregistered citizens must make their way to the Medical Facility.'

'M-m-medical Facility?' Dev stuttered. 'No, no, *no*. I'll need *tools* to fix Boja. His insides are mechanical, like yours.'

Plops was having none of it. He bumped Dev again, nudging him away from the Flember Stream and towards the shadow of the first-floor balconies. Into a network of sleek, white rooms, a jungle of cables strung along the ceilings and all manner of strange-looking equipment half-hidden behind the curtains. More droids awaited them. These droids looked different to Plops. They wore medical smocks and, for some reason, face masks, while a variety of weird and wonderful tools hung out from their side panels.

'What . . . what's going on?' Dev asked, as the floor beneath his feet suddenly started to move, shunting him along like a conveyor belt. 'What are you *doing*?'

Boja stumbled on behind, steadying him-self as the belt struggled to carry his ample weight. A gaggle of medic droids poked and prodded him as he passed, tapping his head, squeezing his eyes.

73

Then one of them jabbed something sharp into his right buttock.

Suddenly Boja's giggles became a bellowing yelp of pain. Flember burst out from his fur, arcing around the room like a lightning bolt. It exploded a few pieces of equipment, which set fire to the curtains. A cluster of fire droids, sirens flashing, emerged from a panel in the wall and rushed to hose it out.

Boja turned around. He looked furious. Upon catching sight of the medic droid who had jabbed him, he swung out his good arm, sending the droid bouncing off a few walls and then out across the glass floor of the atrium.

'What did you just do to Boja?' Dev demanded.

But the medic droids didn't respond. They were too busy clamping an oversized harness around the bear's wrist, inside of which a small flemberthyst crystal started to glow. A series of screens dropped around them, crackling with static, as an outline of the bear flickered up. Dials spun around. Exclamation marks popped in and out. Numbers streamed down around Boja like a waterfall.

The medic droids stared at each other, beeping, as if they were struggling to calculate what was going on.

'Beep! Beep! Boja registers as Prime flember,' Plops announced.

74

'Please . . . his arm.' Dev started clambering along the conveyor belt. 'We really only came here to fix his arm!' Suddenly he felt something jab into his own bum. He turned to see another medic droid, nervously hovering with a needle.

'PROCEDURE MUST BE FOLLOWED.' Plops clamped a smaller harness around Dev's wrist. Something scratched against his skin. He peered at the tiny glowing flemberthyst crystal inside it, before realizing what he was looking at.

It was his own flember.

'You have also been registered as having Prime flember,' Plops announced. 'All medical solutions will be made available to you.'

'Finally!' Dev growled. His patience was starting to wear thin. 'Then would you *please* lend me a Winchdriver, an Optylopop, a Cogglesnotch, and a Root-pinioned Fisplestaw.'

'Oh, Dev. We can offer you more than that.' A tall, elegantly dressed lady glided along beside them. Dev recognized her from the race, from the screens hanging above it. *Grace Neverwhere.* Her long, velvety robes trailed along behind, carrying her across the floor as if she were a ghost.

His eyes, however, were drawn to the strange, glowing skull she was holding.

Grace smiled affectionately.

'You've been working with sticks and stones,' she said. 'Now you're here, Dev, we can offer you the *stars*.'

9

All the Flember You Want

The conveyor belt shunted to a halt, bringing Dev stumbling onto his knees before a large metal door. It too was strapped with elaborate locks and hinges, just like the door on Prosperity's outskirts.

'I go by many names around here,' Grace said, stepping in front of the door. 'Some call me the First Pioneer. But you, Dev, you should call me Grace.'

'Grayss,' Boja mumbled, as he bumped up behind Dev.

For all Grace was saying, however, Dev still couldn't help but stare at the skull she was holding. Up close it looked absolutely battered. Its eye sockets were dark and hollow, its teeth broken, and the large, spiky golden crown sat upon it was so old, so weathered, it looked as if it had melted onto the skull itself. But it was the things around it that fascinated Dev the most. The metal plates, the wires, the aerials. The cluster of mechanical parts that seemed to be lighting the skull up from the inside.

'I . . . I just need to fix Boja's arm,' Dev replied, unable to look away. Then he caught himself. 'Hang on, how do you know my name?'

'Oh, now you're registered we know a *lot* about you.' Grace winked. 'But there is one thing I don't know. I don't know how you're getting through our *locks*.'

Dev sheepishly reached into his pocket, and pulled out his key.

'REALLY?' Grace stared at it admiringly. 'And that works?'

Dev reached up towards the door's central orb, and slipped his key in behind it. *Click!* Clacklescrew. Flemberthysts started to glow along the cables. *Click!* Rufflehinge. *Click! Click! Click!* Knucklebolts! Farplenuts! Lock-jawed whistlesprings! Suddenly every arm on the door was unlocking, as bright, flickering flember flowed towards the orb.

And then, CLUNK, the door itself heaved open.

'How intriguingly simple!' Grace yelped with delight. 'What an inventive mind you have. I'm *so* glad you're finally here!'

'*Finally?*' Dev asked, still a little wary. 'Did . . . did you know we were coming?'

'We haven't had anything sent through from Darkwater for quite some time,' Grace replied, admiring the large, swaying Boja in front of her. 'We were due a delivery of *some* description.'

She swept in through the door, leading Dev into quite the most impressive room he had ever seen. Its walls were tall, majestic, its ceiling curved and arched like a cathedral. Thick white cables hung down like tree vines, all of them pulsing with flember and casting an eerie

flickering glow across the room.

'I also know *why* you both came to Prosperity.' Grace swept in, a fluster of medic droids bumping around her. 'I know you're trying to save your Eden Tree. I know you want to borrow some of Prosperity's flember.'

'H . . . how do you know about the Eden Tree . . . ?' Dev started.

'Look around you,' Grace gleefully interrupted. 'We have *plenty* of flember to spare.'

Boja loudly FLOMP-ed down beside them. He was looking weaker now, swaying and giggling to himself.

'Well, we would *love* to borrow some flember,' Dev said, still a little unsure of how Grace could know so much. 'But I need to fix Boja first and, well, I was hoping you might be able to help me.'

'We'll do it all at the same time!' Grace carefully placed the skull on top of a plinth, then grabbed a stick of bright-green fluffy candy from one of the droids. She crouched down before Boja, and wafted it back and forth in front of him. 'Boja? Are you hungry? We call this flogglefloss, and I can assure you it's ninety-nine per cent *sugar.*'

Boja's head lifted, his big black nose twitching as it caught the sweet, sugary smell. His nostrils flared, his eyes bulged, and suddenly he was drifting back onto his feet as if lured by a spell. CHOMP! His entire mouth consumed Grace's arm, right up to the elbow. She carefully, graciously slid it back out from between his lips.

A bare stick was still clenched between her fingers.

'There's plenty more,' she said, leading Boja towards a wide metal archway in the centre of the room. It had been lined with sticks of flogglefloss as if they were bunches of flowers. Boja skipped between them, plucking at the flogglefloss, nibbling it between his lips like he was eating carefully cut sandwiches at a garden party.

Suddenly, a bright white light beamed down upon

him, freezing Boja to the spot.

'What's that light for?' Dev panicked.

Grace picked up the skull once more. It hummed, flickered, its eye sockets glowing and then, as if the skull had commanded it, a cable FLOMP-ed down behind Dev. He yelped with surprise as the cable started slithering between his boots and on towards the archway.

'I'm doing what you wanted,' Grace calmly stated. 'I'm

fixing your bear.'

Upon reaching Boja, the cable reared up, then lunged, wrapping itself around his ankle. Another writhed around behind him, grabbing his wrist. Another went up his nose. The fourth cable . . . Dev didn't see where it went, but by the startled look in Boja's bulging eyes he could certainly take a guess.

'The glowing skull controls the cables!' Dev gasped.

'The skull controls *Prosperity*.' Grace watched Dev's reaction with delight. 'And *I* control the skull.'

Waves of flember pulsed along the cables then sank beneath Boja's fur, crackling and sparkling through his entire body. It glowed so bright it transformed him into an X-ray of himself. Suddenly Dev could see all of Boja's metallic bones, his hand-sewn organs, big lumps of flogglefloss sinking from his spring-loaded jaws down into his gurgling stomach sac.

'Oh, Dev, you've done remarkable work here already,' Grace admired. 'Quite, quite remarkable. To build such a creature from junk. To make it all move with just an old fluxator circuit for a brain, and then to bring it to life with a pumping . . . gold . . . heart.'

Glowing screens PLINK-PLINK-PLINK-ed out around the skull. Upon them Dev could see a network of bright, glowing lines running through Boja's internal workings.

He stepped a little closer.

'That's Boja's flember,' Dev gasped.

'We've connected him directly to the Flember Stream,' Grace said. She gently held onto Dev's hand, and lifted it towards one of the screens. 'And we're going to use it to fix him. Or rather, you are. Do you see, right there, the break in his arm? How the break is blocking the flow of his flember?'

Dev nodded.

'Well, we should be able to give Boja a blast of flember and push right through that break.'

Dev nervously hovered his fingers over the glowing buttons. 'So, to give Boja more flember . . . do I just touch the screen?'

'Just touch the screen.' Grace guided his hand. Instantly Boja lit up like a firework, great flames of flember dancing out from his fur.

His eyes seemed to widen in alarm.

The medic droids scuttled further back into the shadows.

'Carefully.' Grace gripped Dev's wrist tighter and lifted his hand away. 'Take your time, Dev. Flember must be *carefully* controlled.'

Dev nodded, closely studying the screen. 'Well, let's see. That's Boja's flaxion joint,' he said. 'The raxion joint too. Pringlets one, fine, two, fine . . . three and four, they're the broken ones.'

He cautiously slid his finger along them.

Flember rippled through Boja's body.

Boja's face softened in delight.

Then, CLUNK! Dev heard one of Boja's metallic bones slot back into place.

CLUNK! CLUNK CLUNK!

'Did I . . . did I fix him?' Dev marvelled.

Boja was still frozen mid-flogglefloss-chomp, but his once floppy arm was starting to move. It stretched out in front of him. His fingers clenched and unclenched.

'I'd say you did,' Grace said. 'If we can tap into someone's flember, Dev, then we can reach anywhere inside their body. We can ride it towards the broken bones, the burst valves, the beating heart. Flember is our doorway into the soul itself!'

'So . . . could we give Boja a little extra flember now?' Dev asked. 'Just enough to carry back home, just enough to bring our Eden Tree back to life?'

'Of course!' Grace gestured to the screens. 'Help yourselves. This is why you came all this way, isn't it?'

With an excitement in his heart and thoughts of home popping into his head, Dev leant towards the screen for a second time. He slowly, slow-w-w-ly, slid his fingers up, watching as the cables around Boja stiffened, their flemberthysts pulsating with light.

And as they glowed brighter, Boja's flember levels started to rise.

One hundred per cent flember.

One hundred and five per cent flember.

One hundred and *ten* per cent flember.

Boja's whole body glowed brighter, and brighter. Flember danced across his fur, crackling like a firework around him from his head to his bottom and back again.

One hundred and twenty per cent flember.

One hundred and thirty.

'We're doing it, Boja!' Dev gasped. 'We're borrowing flember from the Flember Stream!'

Suddenly a cluster of exclamation marks flashed across the screens. Alarms sounded. Medic droids hid. Boja's flember level started to sink dramatically. One hundred per cent. Ninety. Eighty. Dev looked up in horror as Boja started to thrash and writhe around inside the archway.

'HWOOOOOAR-R-R-R-RGHHH!' he boomed.

'What's happened?' Dev yelped. 'What's WRONG?'

Grace jabbed at the screens, plinking away the warning symbols as soon as they appeared. 'His body's not strong enough to hold any more flember,' she stated calmly. 'You've overloaded him too many times before, and now his circuits are frying.'

'HELP HIM!' Dev begged.

'He's already been very damaged,' Grace replied. 'He'll need a lot more fixing than I thought.' She swiped her fingers across one last screen. As she did, the cables slackened. The screens flickered away. The beam of light

suddenly switched off, and a huge, exhausted bear once again slumped face first into the ground.

'Boja,' Dev cried, skidding alongside him. He yanked away the cables. 'Boja, are you all right?'

'Hngrghh,' Boja mumbled, as sharp crackles of flember fizzed across his fur.

'What is it? What are you saying?'

A weak smile spread across Boja's lips. 'Hunnnngry,' he groaned.

10
A Buffet of Delights

The dining hall, situated upon the second floor of the Spire, was a grand, lavishly decorated affair. Its walls were covered with purple wallpaper, furry to the touch, punctuated by a succession of huge round windows overlooking the city. Glass chandeliers hung from the ceilings. They caught the light of the Flember Stream running up through the atrium, scattering a patchwork of twinkling lights across the Prime citizens while they sat at their tables and ate their meals.

Plops the droid was first out of the elevator, followed by Dev.

'Here you go,' Dev whispered, helping a decidedly wobbly Boja stagger out across the bridge. 'Grace said they

do food here. This should help you feel a lot better . . .'

Suddenly Boja's nostrils caught a whiff of something. Instantly he perked up. His nose twitched, drifting him, as if in a dream, between the long tables, past the other Primes, past the droids dressed up like waiters, and over to the serving trolleys stacked against the wall. His eyes opened as wide as they would go as he saw all the sizzling delights on offer. Beef marmalade. Chopped chipplenut stew. Lashings of creamed goat goulash. And that was only the first course. Sandwiches carved into the neatest little triangles. Rumblepounds, fingerbobs and chewy nupple twists – but miniature versions of them, delicately laid out as if they were pieces of art. Glazed chicken sticks, chofflegulps and watermelon cubes, all arranged in a variety of sculptures. And in amongst them a line of perfectly sized blobs of sauce: green sauce, pink sauce, every colour sauce in a neat line, each topped by fiddly clusters of finely shredded vegetables.

It all looked delicious, and needlessly fussy at the same time.

'Breakfascht,' Boja drooled. He stopped a nearby waiter droid, politely took its tray and tipped a plate of wobbling pink jellies into his mouth. He chewed – just once – before swallowing. His lips smacked as if he was trying to place the flavours. Then he grabbed another tray and swallowed it just the same.

'RULE 632!' Plops announced, whizzing alongside and producing a fork from its front panel. 'All Prime citizens MUST use cutlery in the canteen.'

Dev plucked the fork for himself. 'Boja's a more . . . *hands-on* sort of bear.' He grinned, scooping a forkful of minced ruffle delight into his mouth and closing his eyes to savour the flavours. It was sweet, chewy, tangy and warm. Compared to the food he'd been eating in Darkwater – even the gritcake he had been offered on

the outskirts – this tasted *heavenly*.

'Oh, Brianne and Rails would love this! Much better than that weird gritcake they were eating,' he chuckled, shoofing the backpack from his shoulders, opening it up, and shovelling lumps of food inside. Whistlechips, half-moons, sugar-coated fizzlumps, all swept from the table and piled in beside the flember book. 'I'll take some back for them to say thank you for all their help!'

'That's PRIME food,' someone growled from the table beside him. Dev turned to see Ralto – huge, hulking Ralto, his white hair smeared grey with what looked like engine oil. As Ralto stood, Dev saw his armour had been fixed up, buffed and polished, with all the dents hammered out. He even had new claws.

Bigger claws.

'So I suggest,' Ralto continued, 'you leave it where it belongs.'

An anger rushed through Dev's veins. 'You broke Boja's ARM!' he yelled. 'You HURT BOJA!'

'HURT me,' Boja huffed, using his newly fixed arm to stuff fistfuls of freshwater prawns into his mouth. They bulged in his cheeks, their frilly pink tails hanging from his lips.

The second racer, Sienna, stood up beside Ralto. Her armour too had been improved, sharp splints fixed along her arms as if she could slice a ham from twenty metres away.

Her cold blue eyes once again stared Dev down, as the lights upon her armour pulsed with each breath.

And all of a sudden, Dev realized what those lights were.

'Flemberthysts,' he gasped, reaching out towards them. 'You all have *flemberthysts* built into your armour.'

'Don't be stupid, they're just lights.' Ralto growled, pushing Dev's hand away. 'Something to entertain the crowds.'

The third racer, Esco, walked out from the kitchens in his own newly polished armour. He walked silently between them all, swished up his cape, sat down at the table, swept his flock of short white hair to one side, straightened his pointy moustache, and slurped at his flask of drink.

'Don't bother trying to explain, Ralto,' Esco said. 'They're sewer rats, they don't understand how things work around here.'

'We're Prime, just like you,' Dev growled back, holding up the glowing harness on his wrist. 'See? Both of us. They tested our flember when we came in. Even though . . . I'm not entirely sure what Prime means.'

Esco snorted. 'It means the best of the best.'

'YEAH!' Ralto clanged his huge claws against his chest. 'Our flember is superior to everyone's outside the boundary. We're stronger, smarter, cleverer-er . . .'

'We're just *better*,' Esco finished.

'But that doesn't make sense!' Dev replied. 'Flember doesn't change. It isn't better or worse depending on who holds it. Flember is *universal*.'

Esco snorted, took another sip of his drink, then glanced at Dev over his plastered nose. 'Look around you, sewer rat. Prime flember *built* this city. Prime flember put food on the end of your fork.' He reached over, grabbed the fork from Dev's hand, jabbed it into the pile of minced ruffle delight, and chomped down a mouthful. 'Prime flember brings us a way of life far more comfortable than the Lessers could even dream of.'

'Lessers?' Dev asked.

'You'll have met them on the outskirts,' Esco smirked. 'Terrible creatures. Dirty clothes, dusty hair, grunting like savages. Lessers have . . . *inferior* flember to Primes. It's not their fault, of course, but it is important they know their place.' He leant back in his chair. 'That's what the race was supposed to prove,' he growled. 'Until you two fell onto the track and ruined it.'

'GUHHHHHHH!' Boja suddenly cried. He had given up trying to eat prawns by the fistful, and instead used his tongue to scoop them out. The bowl, however, was carved of ice, and his long, wet tongue had become stuck to the inside of it.

'BEEP! Rule 632! All Prime citizens MUST use cutlery!' Plops barked.

But it was a little too late for serving forks. Boja had become gripped by panic. As he pulled at the bowl he yanked his tongue out further, and further, far further than Dev remembered ever having designing it to stretch. Only when it stretched as long as his arms did the ice bowl finally let go with a loud SCHLU-U-U-U-UPPP,

sending Boja tumbling backwards over a table and crushing a number of waiter droids beneath his sizeable buttocks. Dev rushed around to grab Boja's waggling legs, but as he did he noticed something rather odd.

There were puffs of smoke spilling out from Boja's feet.

The smoke then sputtered into sparks – bright blue sparks – spinning out lines of flember to form what looked like boots around his legs. Within an instant, flames had blasted out from the soles, propelling Boja into a backwards somersault and then SLAMMING him against the wall. He groaned, clutched his head and staggered back onto his feet. The boots, however, were still blazing, each step bouncing him a few centimetres above the floor.

'Boja, what . . . what's happening?' Dev asked, hardly able to believe what he was seeing.

'BOUNCY!' A huge grin spread across Boja's face, as he bounced a step forwards. Then another. And another. Suddenly he was bouncing between the tables, denting the ceiling with his head each time but not seeming to mind at all. 'OW!' he cheered. 'OW! OW OW!'

One of the dining hall's many chandeliers brought Boja's fun to an end. He collided into it with a loud CRASH, pulling it from the ceiling and dragging it down into a rather large raspberry pannacotta. Before he could even take a mouthful, however, his flember boots fired up again.

With a loud WOO-O-O-O-O-OSHHHH, he was propelled along the table, dragging clinking chandelier bits through row upon row of elaborate dishes, his mouth opening wide as he devoured every delicacy in his path. Before crashing, messily, into the three Prime racers at the end.

Boja's feet sputtered.

His flember crackled back down inside his fur.

A flurry of waiter droids whizzed around the dining hall, scooping up the mess. Esco was the first back on his feet, as he wiped a clump of home-cured gobblemeats from his armour.

'Your monster may be Prime,' he seethed. 'But it doesn't belong here. Neither of you do.'

Dev was about to apologize for the mess Boja had

caused, to tell the Primes they had no intention of staying here any longer than necessary, when suddenly a loud HON-N-N-N-NKKK made everyone in the dining hall jump.

'BEEP!' Plops barked. 'Will all non-racing Primes please make their way to the viewing platform!'

A chatter of excitement rippled through the other diners as they scraped their chairs back. 'W . . . what's going on?' Dev asked. 'Where's everyone going?'

Ralto removed the upturned plate of cocklespritzles from his head, readjusted his armour, and followed Esco and Sienna towards the elevator. 'It's the second race,' he grunted.

'*Second* race?' Dev asked.

'BEST OF THREE!' Esco snapped. 'And there's not a chance we're losing *this* one.'

11
The Glowing Skull

The third floor of the Spire served as a viewing platform. Its huge glass walls looked out across the concourse, the gardens, the writhing cables of the boundary, opening up at the front into an elegant balcony for those who wanted the very best view of all. Seats had already been laid out by the droids, and the ample bottoms of the Prime citizens were starting to fill them.

At the very front sat Grace, the First Pioneer. Her seat was lavish, a throne gilded with decoration. She had changed her clothes to match it. Now she wore a long, flowing robe of gold-embroidered satin, decorated with compass symbols, puffing up around her cheeks as if

to frame her face.

Plops led Dev and Boja out onto the balcony. Despite his sizeable breakfast, Boja's sudden, bizarre, outburst of flember had weakened him again. He was limping now, his eyes aching to fall asleep, his whole body heavy and uncomfortable.

'The bear still doesn't look well.' Grace frowned, patting the empty seats beside her. 'Perhaps he'll need more than just food to get him back to normal.'

'Something weird happened.' Dev sighed. 'His feet blasted out flember and, well, I don't know how to fix it. I don't want to risk hurting him again.'

'We have . . . other ways to fix him.' Grace smiled. 'But do you mind if we talk about it after the race? This is quite an important one, you see. If the Lessers win this race as well as the first one, then, well then they'll have won two out of three. By our own rules that would mean we must share Prosperity's flember with them, and all the Primes sat behind us will be very, *very* unhappy about that.'

Dev turned his head to the other Prime citizens.

They all stared nervously back.

'While we hold the skull, however, we still control the flember.' Grace picked up the skull from the small table beside her, stood, and carried it towards the edge of the balcony.

The skull's eyes started to glow.

Somewhere far in the distance Dev heard a loud rumbling noise. He followed Grace, and looked out to see huge clouds of dust billowing up beyond the boundary. Slowly, the old stone houses of the outskirts rose behind it. One by one they formed a tiered stand of rooftops and, as before, the Lessers crowded upon them. Cheers were cried. Flags billowed. Bufflechips were chomped.

Only for the crowd to then part, as three racers stepped through.

Brianne was first to appear on the screens. Her armour still looked old and battered, but even from here Dev could see she had changed it. *Improved* it. Her top half was now protected by a metal roll-cage, and a row of hydraulic pumps had been added around her waist. A twin rocket-pack had been welded onto her back. One of her arms now wore the claw salvaged from Ralto's armour. The screens zoomed in on the stone compass she'd won in the first race. Now it had been dipped in silver and embedded into her chest plate.

'There she is!' Dev excitedly yelled. 'Look, Boja, it's Brianne!'

Boja took an armful of bobbly orange canapés from a passing waiter droid and stood, only to find the chair still wedged firmly onto his bottom. 'BREE-ANN!' he mumbled, waddling towards the balcony and sitting back down beside Dev. Together they watched excitedly as the two other Lesser racers – Pipo and Dollop – joined Brianne on the racetrack. And then the track itself started to split apart, whole sections pulled away by cables, gently carrying the racers down until they could step onto the grass of Prosperity's gardens.

'Everything in Prosperity *moves!*' Dev marvelled, turning to Grace, only for his eyes to once again fall upon the skull. Its ebbing, fluorescent light felt strange to look at. Hypnotizing, almost.

A loud cheer from the Primes snapped him out of his thoughts, as images of Esco, Ralto and Sienna appeared across the screens. Dev leant over the balcony railings to see the three Prime racers standing upon the very edge of the concourse. They looked proud. Determined. With only a little bit of food still left in their hair.

Esco raised a salute towards the viewing platform. 'For Prime,' he declared. 'For Prosperity. For *you*, Mother!'

Grace nodded gracefully.

'They're your children?' Dev exclaimed, then clonked his helmet, suddenly noticing the white-haired likeness.

'They're the best of the best,' Grace replied. 'Of *course* they're my children!'

Sienna and Ralto followed with more salutes, as the lights across their armour blazed and they revelled in the rapturous applause from the Primes. Then, rather ceremonially, they each leapt into the air and sailed gracefully down into the gardens.

'The first race was about speed.' Grace stood alongside Dev. 'This second race will test their *agility*.' She tilted the skull down towards the gardens. A cacophony of cracks, crunches and creaks rose from between the trees, followed by whole sections of the ground itself. Lawns, rockeries, shrubberies, all of them lifted into the air upon thick strands of glowing cable.

They rose like platforms around the perimeter of the gardens. Then, with a loud rumble, more sections of ground started to lift, these rising higher. Then more, higher still, and more, together forming a spiral staircase of platforms, leading up to the statue on an incredibly high column at the very centre of the gardens.

The statue.

Although he couldn't quite see its face, this statue looked different from the one of Grace. It was tall

and stocky, its thick, strong hands cradling a floating sphere of glass, inside of which had been encased a single, solitary flower.

Grace's face beamed across the screens once again. 'Good citizens of Prosperity,' she announced. A cheer went up from both the Lessers along the boundary, and the Primes inside the Spire. 'The gardens are now out of bounds as we gather for our next race, to honour the great work of our Second Pioneer. I may have built Prosperity, but *he* brought us flember!'

'So, it was *him* that found the

Flember Stream?' Dev whispered.

Grace thrust the skull high above her head, its eyes blazing brighter than ever. 'YOU ALL KNOW THE RULES!' she declared. 'Racers must ascend the platforms to reach the statue, and then take its flower. Whoever claims it, whoever holds the Second Pioneer's whitedrop, will be declared the WINNER!'

Dev watched the racers, both Lesser and Prime, step towards their nearest platforms.

He gulped nervously.

Then HON-N-N-N-NKK, a loud klaxon shook through Prosperity, confetti filled the skies, a great cheer went up from both crowds, and before Dev could even take a breath the second race had started.

12
The Race for the Whitedrop

Dev glanced up at the screens to see Esco take a huge leap onto the first platform. There he paused, soaking in the Prime crowd's adulation. Ralto tried to follow, only for Sienna to leap onto his head as if it were a springboard and somersault up alongside Esco like a highly trained acrobat.

The screens then showed what was happening on the other side of the gardens. The Lesser armour may not have been as sleek or as flashy as Prime, but it was holding together well, and it carried

each racer
up onto the
rocky terrain
of their first
platforms. Brianne,
wasting no time,
then slapped the
twin rocket-pack on
her back. It belched
out a large plume of grey
smoke and, FWOOOOSH,
sent her flying up in a long arc of
smoke, only to splash down into a puddle two platforms
higher up.

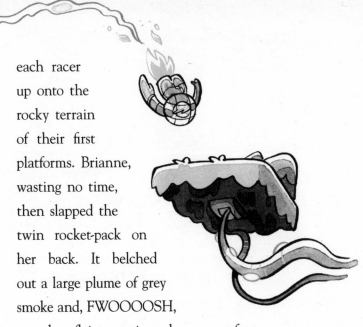

Even from here Dev could hear the cheers of the
Lesser crowd beyond the boundary, and it brought a
grin to his face. But then, on the screens, he caught
sight of someone in amongst the crowd, someone carefully slipping down onto the racetrack, creeping across
it, then lowering themselves down into the treetops. It
was a boy, barely older than Dev. His clothes were torn
and his purple hair was ruffled over his eyes.

Strapped to his back he carried a rather oversized
sword.

'SANTORO!' Dev shrieked in excitement, before clamping his hands over his mouth. He nudged Boja in the ribs. Boja choked on his fifteenth fistful of fish eggs, then caught sight of what Dev was looking at.

'SAN—' the bear boomed, only for Dev to swiftly reach out a hand and pinch his lips shut. '— tmpschmph.'

'Shhhh! They can't know he's here!' Dev whispered. 'What if they don't think he's Prime flember? They'll kick him out!' He gripped Boja's paw tightly. 'Boja, we have to get to him first!'

As discreetly as he could, Dev led the big red bear with a chair wedged on his bottom away from the balcony. Fortunately Grace, Plops and all the rest of the Primes seemed absorbed in watching the race, and only a few passing waiter droids saw them slip into the elevator.

'Santoro must have come looking for us! He must have left Eden and gone through the Wildening, just like we did!' Dev breathlessly exclaimed as they rode down through the lights of the Flember Stream. 'But he made it! On his own! He made it all the way to Prosperity!'

Pride swelled inside Dev's chest.

'He's really strong, my brother.' He beamed. 'Santoro can handle *anything*.'

The elevator couldn't carry them down fast enough, but when it finally arrived in the gardens Dev and Boja stepped back out into a cacophony of noise. Dev looked up and saw that Ralto was still struggling to clamber onto the first platform, but high above him the other racers were clanging, puffing and blasting towards the top. Brianne, in particular, was easy to spot. Her armour whistled the loudest, heaving her down into a crouch before sending her riding upwards and landing her just a few platforms away from the statue.

'She's doing really well,' Dev cheered. 'But this is one race we're keeping out of. We have other things to—'

'DEV!' Santoro yelled, running between the cables that held up the platforms.

Dev squeaked with another noise he didn't know he could make, then pelted as fast as his legs could carry him. 'Santoro, you FOUND us!' he cried, flinging himself towards his brother and wrapping his arms tightly around his shoulders. Then his smile cracked. Tears wobbled in his eyes. 'I . . . I didn't mean for us to be away so long!' he whimpered.

'It's OK, Dev,' Santoro whispered. 'I found you. That's all that matters.'

'SCHANTORO!' Boja ran towards them, bottom still wedged inside a posh chair, arms outstretched, ready to give them both the squeezing of a lifetime, before he tripped on a clump of mud and stumbled onto his face.

And then his eyelids closed.

And he had a little nap.

'Boja's not well,' Dev replied. 'His insides, they're . . . they're broken. But Grace, the First Pioneer, she said she can fix him . . .'

Suddenly there came a loud explosion from above. Dev looked up to see Brianne clinging to the side of the statue by her oversized claw, her twin rocket-pack consumed by a bright orange fire. Esco held onto the other side of the statue, staring in horror at the thick jagged line CRA-A-A-ACKING its way down the full length of its column.

'We have to go!' Dev shouted, as both he and Santoro dragged Boja's face out of the dirt. Boja yawned, raised his eyebrows at the two brothers hopping frantically around him and then finally, FINALLY, noticed the huge clumps of rock raining down around them.

With what sounded like a bark, Boja's ears pinned back, he leapt to his feet, spun on his heels, and scooped Dev and Santoro under each arm. Then he was gone, racing as fast as he could towards the boundary. 'R-r-r-un to the s-s-s-side!' Dev yelled, as the looming shadow of the column chased them across the grass. But Boja was panicking too much to hear. Panicking so much, in fact, that flember started to crackle across his fur, spiralling around his arms, his legs. His big bulgy eyes started to spin and then, with a SPUT-SPUT-SPUT, bright blue flames blasted out from his feet just like before.

FWOOOSH-H-H-H-H-H! Boja and the two brothers were rocketed forwards into a somersault, spinning just clear of the statue's head as it crashed into the lawns behind them. They flew straight into a clump of

particularly thorny bracken, Boja somehow remaining upright, wobbling on the unsteady legs of his chair with Dev and Santoro safely tucked under his arms.

Bits of statue fell from the sky and slammed down into the ground, closely followed by Esco, then Brianne, then Dollop and Pipo. And then Ralto, finally falling off the first platform and flailing helplessly on his back like an upturned rumblebug.

In fact, the only racer who seemed quite untouched by it all was Sienna. She strode purposefully through the dust, between the other racers, stepping over the ruins of the statue before reaching down and plucking the white-drop from its hands.

HON-N-N-N-N-N-NKKK!

The Prime crowd went crazy, cheering and whooping upon the viewing platform as Sienna's face flashed across the screens.

'We have a WINNER!' Grace appeared once again. 'Good people of Prosperity, the second Pioneer Race has been won by a PRIME!'

More cheers from the Primes. A low rumble of boos from the crowd beyond the boundary.

'One race won by Lesser, one race won by Prime.' Grace smiled, her eyes looking down from the screens as if she was staring straight at Dev and Santoro. 'Well then, it looks like we'll have to decide it with a third!'

13
Santoro

'Boja, are you OK?' Dev squeezed out from under Boja's big red arm and checked the bear for injuries. He lifted his heavy eyelids. He flicked his big black nose. He pulled his finger until a fart PARP-ed loudly out from between Boja's buttocks.

'Phew,' Dev sighed. 'I think he's fine.'

Santoro wrestled himself free, dusting off his floppy hair. 'Trust you to end up somewhere so *dangerous*,' he said, just as Brianne hauled herself from amongst the cables with a loud GA-A-A-A-ASP! Her armour was singed and smoking, her face smeared with oil and dirt, but she seemed to be all right. That is until Ralto loomed up behind her and wrenched his old claw from her arm.

116

'That's PRIME technology,' he coughed, pulling it away in a shower of sparks. 'Not for the likes of *you!*'

'Leave her alone!' Dev stepped out defiantly. He reached out a hand to help Brianne onto her feet.

'Dev, you made it inside the boundary!' She grinned, wiping the mud from her lips. 'And Boja, did you—'

'FICKSCHED!' Boja raised both arms as he wobbled in his chair.

'His arm's OK now,' Dev replied. 'Although, the rest of him is a bit—'

'You were so close!' Pipo cried as he and Dollop clambered over clumps of dirt and rock.

'We nearly *won!*' Dollop clung onto Brianne, as they held each other upright.

'We'll win the next one.' Brianne winked at Dev.

Suddenly the elevator doors opened up behind them,

and a swarm of droids hovered out. These were police droids, red flashing lights on their heads, WEE-OO-WEE-OO sirens wailing, as they bumped the Lesser racers across the gardens and back towards the boundary.

'THE LESSERS WILL WIN THE NEXT ONE!' Brianne shouted back to the watching Primes. 'YOU JUST SEE IF WE DON'T!'

Sienna rolled her eyes, tucked the whitedrop into her helmet, then strode inside the open elevator. Ralto followed, dragging his spare claw through the dirt. The two of them then waited for Esco, who, upon seeing Dev and Santoro, readjusted his torn cape and grimaced. 'I see more rats are getting into the city,' he snarled.

Santoro snarled right back.

As the elevator carried the Prime racers away, the cables around the gardens started to shake, pulling the platforms back down towards the ground. The moss-covered rocks clunked in alongside the pools, the trees slotted back across the lawns. Apart from the destroyed statue and its column lying straight across the ground like the broken hand of a clock, the gardens soon looked as serene as they had before.

Dev watched it all in absolute amazement.

'How *did* you both end up in a place like this?' Santoro huffed, folding his arms across his chest.

Dev swung a broad smile around to his brother. 'Oh, isn't Prosperity amazing!' he exclaimed, he-e-e-eaving the chair from Boja's bottom. 'Quite different from Darkwater. We found the Flember Stream there but then, well, we lost it, so Prosperity was next on the map.' He paused. 'Wait, did *you* go to Darkwater?'

'I did.' Santoro raised an eyebrow. 'And I heard you flooded their quarry!'

'I guess we did do that,' Dev mumbled.

'But you also brought *food* to Darkwater, decent food, and you showed them how to grow it.' There was admiration in Santoro's voice. It was reluctant, perhaps, but it was there. 'You did well, Dev.'

Dev's cheeks flushed.

'So you came here looking for more flember?' Santoro asked.

'We FOUND more flember!' Dev pointed over to the

119

Flember Stream as it shone up into the Spire. 'Look at it, Santoro. Isn't it beautiful?'

The light of the Flember Stream twinkled in Santoro's eyes. 'So this is flember?' he marvelled. 'This is the thing you've been chasing after . . .'

Plops suddenly hovered out from inside the glass elevator. 'BEEP! RULE 001! All citizens must have their flember registered!'

Santoro jumped back, pulling his sword out and swinging it towards the droid. 'It's . . . it's OK,' Dev said, lifting his harness to show Santoro the glowing flemberthyst inside it. 'This is just what they do here. It's how they decide if you can stay.' He nervously reached out and lowered Santoro's blade. 'So let's not give them *any* reason to throw you out.'

Santoro stood on the Medical Facility conveyor belt, his huge sword sheathed across his shoulders, growling at any medic droids who tried to take it off him. Only now, walking alongside, did Dev notice all the marks across Santoro's body. The scratches across his skin. The bruises along his legs.

'Did you get those in the Wildening?' Dev asked sheepishly.

Santoro cast a weary eye down at his injuries. 'The rumours were all true about that place,' he muttered. 'It's dark, and it moves. And it *hunts*.' He caught sight of the three blackened scratches across Dev's arm. 'Did it get you too?'

'Well, yes, a *wolf* bit me. But I had Boja to keep me safe.' Dev looked fondly over to the far corner of the facility, where Boja had lifted Plops upside down and was shaking it as if there might be a toy rattling around inside.

'Well, you both did well to make it thro-O-O-O-U-G-H!' Santoro roared out in pain, swinging around and drawing his sword towards whichever medic droid had just injected a needle into his bottom. Another droid took its chance, clamping the harness onto Santoro's wrist and hurrying away to a safe distance.

'That's your flember,' Dev smiled, pointing to the glowing flemberthyst inside the harness.

Santoro's face softened. 'My flember?' he gasped.

'PRIME!' Plops announced, as all manner of screens

popped up around Santoro and detailed every inch of his body. Santoro cast his eyes across them, unsure of what he was looking at.

'Prime flember, just like me, and Boja.' Dev smiled with relief. 'Santoro, you can stay inside Prosperity!'

Santoro stared back at him. 'We're not *staying*,' he said. 'You came here to get some flember. Well, let's go get it, and then we can leave.'

'Of . . . of course, we *will*.' Dev nodded. 'I just need to fix Boja first, so he can carry it. He's really not well. Something's gone wrong inside his—'

He turned round to look for Boja.

But Boja had gone.

And he had taken Plops with him.

14
The Library

'BOJA!' Dev skidded out across the glass floor of the atrium. 'BOJA, WHERE ARE YOU?'

'RULE 451!' came an irritated voice from the next level up. 'Do not – BZZT! – do NOT eat the droids!'

'Why can I hear crunching metal?' Santoro asked.

Dev grabbed Santoro by the wrist and yanked him back into the elevator. Together they rode through the Flember Stream, up to the first floor.

Where Dev spotted Boja sitting on the bridge.

Idly chewing Plops between his big teeth.

'BOJA!' Dev stepped out of the elevator. 'Boja, stop

chewing Plops!'

One of Boja's eyes turned to look at Dev. The other remained half-closed. He looked a sorry sight. Every breath he took seemed slow and laboured, each one swaying him, back and forth, upon his big saggy bottom.

'I'm noph . . . oh-kay . . .' Boja sighed.

'I know you're not OK,' Dev winced. 'But we're going to *fix* you, Boja. Grace says she can help. Together, we're going to make you feel well again.'

'BZZZZZZT! INITIATE SELF-DEFENCE!' Plops announced. Suddenly a fizz of electricity shot through it, lighting the droid up like a lantern and sending a short, sharp shock across Boja's whole body. He yelped, dropping Plops to the ground, much to the surprise of the beeping reception droids below.

'Boja!' Dev shouted.

'SHRIIIIIIIEK!' Boja yelled back, scrambling onto his

feet and staggering backwards across the bridge. Dev and Santoro raced towards him, which only made the bear panic even more, as he spun round and bolted through a set of wide stone columns.

A long, floating mist of flember trailed behind him.

Santoro gave chase but Dev couldn't stop himself skidding to a halt, just briefly, to realise what he was about to run into.

This was a *library*.

A library filled with *books*.

He could barely believe it. Huge, towering bookcases, stacked as high as the vaulted ceiling, with long gangways gliding between them. A labyrinth of BOOKS. Hundreds, no, thousands of BOOKS.

It was unlike anything he'd ever seen before, but he had little time to admire it. He ran after Santoro who, in turn, was running after the squawks and beeps of whatever library droids Boja was trampling underfoot. Finally, they found him. Propped up at the end of a long line of bookcases. The big, lumpy bear was half-asleep, sparkling with flember, chewing on a rather large volume of poetry.

'What's *wrong* with him?' Santoro puffed, readjusting his floppy hair.

'He's . . . he's malfunctioning. He overloaded and now I don't think his body can regulate his flember.' Dev patted Boja tenderly on the head. 'But Grace was going to help me fix him.'

Santoro sat himself down beside the big sleeping bear. 'Well, maybe you should find her then, Dev.'

Dev nodded. 'Sleep it off,' he whispered into Boja's ear. 'I'll go and get help.'

'Rfsckoggle,' Boja mumbled. His bottom lip dropped open, the poetry book fell out, and with a loud fart the exhausted bear fell asleep again.

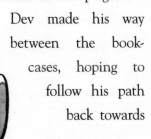

Dev made his way between the bookcases, hoping to follow his path back towards the atrium. His fingers trailed along row upon row of tatty old book spines. 'The Great Pioneer – An Illustrated History,' he read out. 'The Voyage Of The Settlers, Tales From The Homeland, Hufflepig Pie . . . Ten Home-Cooked Recipes For All The Family.'

He couldn't help but be impressed. 'Imagine if old Bumblebuss saw where I was now,' he whispered, thinking of Eden's mayor. 'A whole room full of books. He'd be furious. His big red nose would probably explode.'

He spun around and walked down a different corridor. 'I wonder if my book came from in here,' he mused to himself, as he slid the backpack from his shoulder, opened its buckles, and pulled out the flember book. 'Or at least whatever was once between its covers.'

Dev ran his fingertips across the golden letters studded into its cracked blue leather. 'Flember Island,' he mumbled, looking for a gap upon the shelves where the book cover might have once belonged. 'Well that would be filed under F. So lets see. . . Fishing While At Sea, First Contact Upon the Coast, Flutterskits, How To Spot And Then Avoid Them.'

It was at this point the bookcases ran out, and Dev stumbled into the very centre of the library.

Where he found another statue.

Dev read the nameplate at the statue's feet: 'Cervantes Escobar. Supreme Pioneer. Settler upon Flember Island. Founder of all civilization.'

He gazed at the figure looming high above him. Cervantes Escobar certainly looked as heroic as he sounded, his golden body glinting in the sunlight as he stared purposefully into the distance.

'Magnificent, isn't he?'

Dev jumped at the sound of Grace's voice.

'Oh,' he stuttered. 'I . . . I was just looking for you . . .'

'They say Cervantes Escobar was huge, his shoulders broader than the thickest trees. They say that when he walked the whole island *shook*.' Grace pointed to the front portion of a ship marooned behind the statue. 'He first came here six hundred years ago, in that very ship. Brought with him a vision to create a society of freedom, democracy, to encourage brilliant thinking. Many, many years later we Pioneers would take those ideals and build Prosperity upon them, but Cervantes was the original. He was the Supreme. He started it all.'

Dev smiled politely. 'I was hoping . . . maybe you could help me to fix Boja? He's still acting very strangely.'

'And this, this is his *skull*,' Grace continued, lifting the skull between her hands. 'The very skull of Cervantes Escobar. Adapted a little, of course. We added a few extra parts, and then fine-tuned it.'

As if summoned by the skull's glowing eyes, a roll of thick white cables snaked out from between the book-cases and writhed around the hem of Grace's gown.

Dev stepped back in alarm. 'I . . . I just need help with Boja,' he stuttered. 'You said you could . . .'

'Wouldn't you agree, Dev' – Grace smiled – 'that it's only right that through the skull of our Supreme Pioneer himself, I now control *everything* inside Prosperity.'

'PLEASE – BZZT! – RETURN ALL BORROWED BOOKS WITHIN THREE DAYS!' Plops suddenly announced from behind Dev. The droid looked a little dented – partly from tooth marks, partly from its fall – as it shone a bright beam of light at Dev and scanned his book.

'*Flember Island*, registered title,' Plops declared, as a long metal arm unfolded out from the droid's casing and its pincers grabbed the book from Dev's hands. 'Return to speciality department, case fourteen, shelf thirty-nine immediately.'

'What?' Dev yelped. 'No, no! That . . . that's just the cover. The cover of a *different* book. The flember book, *my* flember book, is hidden inside it.'

Plops wasn't listening. 'Rule 637, all borrowed books – BZZT! – must be returned to the library.' It announced, speeding away between the bookcases.

'That's my BOOK!' Dev yelled, racing after the droid. 'I NEED IT TO GET HOME!'

15
Hidden Secrets

For a floating, malfunctioning bin, Plops was deceptively nimble. It slid between the bookcases with ease, swerving to avoid piles of discarded books before riding up onto a system of ramps, then onto the gangways hanging from the ceiling. Dev lagged behind, eventually climbing the shelves as if they were the steps of a ladder.

'COME BACK!' he cried, pulling himself to the very top. 'PLEASE! I need that BOOK!'

He caught sight of Grace far below. She was watching the chase with amusement. 'You keep saying you'll help me,' Dev muttered. 'But you never quite answer my questions. And you're not helping me *now*.'

'Hurry, it's taking your book!' Grace gestured

after Plops.

'I got this!' Santoro suddenly appeared, running along the top of the bookcase and then leaping across to the next. 'That buzzing lump of metal isn't getting away from ME!'

Once he'd hauled himself up, Dev's steps were a little less steady than his brother. His stomach lurched at every jump across the aisles. Soon, however, the two of them had completed almost a lap of the library in their pursuit of Plops, stopping just a few levels higher than where the chase had begun.

Just above the statue of Cervantes Escobar.

'Give . . . my brother . . . back . . . his BOOK!' Santoro drew his sword and pointed it towards the droid.

'Or at least let me take MY book out of the covers,' Dev begged.

'All borrowed books must be – BZZT – returned to the library,' Plops repeated, hovering in front of the thirty-ninth shelf and lifting the flember book towards a gap.

That is, until an extraordinarily loud noise echoed through the library.

Dev couldn't tell if it was Boja's huge, chesty roar as he decided to join the chase. Or perhaps the loud creaking as the overly tired bear threw himself into a bookcase. Or it may have been that bookcase slamming into the next, which slammed into the next, all of them clattering like giant dominoes towards the statue of Cervantes Escobar.

Or it may have been all those noises, rolled into one.

Boja surfed across the top of the bookcases, tumbling and rolling through a snowstorm of books before being flung against the statue where, in panic, he gripped onto its huge golden head. Only for the statue itself to then start leaning under his weight. An almighty CRE-E-E-EAK echoed through the library as the statue, and Boja, crashed through the surrounding pillars, through the bookcase behind it, and smashed down, through the floor itself.

From their precarious gangway, Dev and Santoro

helped each other down onto the ground, rushed past Grace, and climbed through the giant hole in the library floor. Down they slid, into the dust, and the rubble and the darkness below. 'Boja!' Dev cried, spotting a tuft of red fur buried beneath a mound of books.

It was buttock fur!

Boja's head emerged a little further along.

'Helping,' Boja slurred, still clinging to the detached head of Cervantes Escobar.

'You're not well!' Dev cried, fussing the books away. 'You shouldn't be throwing yourself around like this! Where even *are* we?'

He blinked in the low light. They appeared to be inside a small circular room. Its walls covered with old peeling wallpaper. Mould grew between the cracked tiles of the floor. Surrounding them, were three archways, inside of which had been stacked a cluster of cabinets, boxes and even more boxes.

His curiosity piqued, Santoro slid down onto the floor and edged towards the first arch. 'Hey, Dev,' he called. 'Come and look at all this!'

Keeping a sleepy Boja in his sights, Dev cautiously joined his brother inside the arch. They opened up one of the boxes and took its lid off. There, inside, was a large

sheet of paper folded over and over again.

Dev hauled it out, and spread it across the floor.

'Plans for building the Spire!' he gasped, reaching back inside the box and pulling out more and more papers. Each new page only added to the plans, a little more of the Spire's intricacies, its construction, how everything fitted together. There was no mention of the cables. No mention of the engine. No mention of the flember that powered it all.

But still, it sent an excited spark through Dev's bones.

'Grace said she was the First Pioneer, that she was an architect,' he muttered. 'These must be *her* plans!'

'Hey, Dev, there's more in this one!' Santoro called from the next arch along. He pulled a handful of loose pages out from a drawer and handed them over.

Sketches of pojobo plants, riffledanders and knocking willows. Creatures too. Snot-nosed bats, fisshogs, silverfish and a whole array of animals Dev didn't recognize. The swift, frantic notes and annotations, the handwriting, it all looked so . . . *familiar.*

'The Second Pioneer,' Dev whispered. 'He must have studied flember. His work, his *handwriting*, it looks just like . . .'

His heart raced. He could barely speak the words.

'It looks just like the flember book,' he gasped. 'The Second Pioneer wrote my BOOK!'

He spun round and dived into the huge snoring pile

WHITEDROP

Of all the flowers I have studied, I keep coming back to the WHITEDROP. It's the perfect specimen of nature - it's delicate, yet hardy, it's beautiful, yet small, it represents the fragility of life. And crucially, it demonstrates the holding of flember like no other flower we see, the whitedrop blooms, withers, then blooms again, as if it were taking breath. Somewhere inside this marvellous flower, flember is flowing back and forth in waves.

Petals
stepulae
Finula
Nopples
Finleaves

THE FISSHOG

Glass fibre hairs!

32¹⁰

FRESHWATER
BLOBBLEFISH

SILVERFISH
Not only found in caves, but also

of books behind him. 'I need to find it. I *need* to find it!'

Santoro's attentions, however, had been caught by something else. 'Grace said they'd be running a third race,' he muttered, stepping back from the third arch and staring at the strange symbol nailed above it. 'If the First Pioneer was an architect, and the Second studied flember, what did the Third Pioneer do?'

'It's a Cronklewrench,' Grace called down through the hole in the floor. 'The tool above the arch. It's used for tightening the wingnuts inside the cables.' As she spoke, a swarm of droids rushed alongside her, tumbling down across the books. Their front panels opened, and from inside appeared brushes, pans and nozzled attachments, anything to help clear up the mess.

'Crunklepinch,' Boja murmured, before farting a book up and over Grace's head.

'Cronklewrench,' Grace politely corrected.

'I . . . I'm sorry,' Dev replied. 'About your library, about your statue, about all the mess Boja is causing in Prosperity. He really doesn't mean to cause any trouble. But he's not well, and now I've lost my book, and . . . and . . .' He felt a lump rising in his throat. 'And everything's just going *wrong*!' he sobbed.

Grace placed the skull down, then hauled a rather dented Plops up from the floor. It sparked and garbled, but as she spun it round, Dev saw a book embedded into its back.

'Your book's right here,' she said, smiling kindly towards Boja. '*Somehow*, in all the commotion, it must have become wedged into Plops. So how about I take you to the Development Rooms and we take your book out, then we'll fix Plops *and* Boja all at once, shall we?'

16
Surgery

The Development Rooms were far more than just a few rooms. It was the entire fourth floor of the Spire. And it was filled with the most incredible, mind-bending technology Dev had ever seen. Men and women in lab coats rushed around firing rockets, playing with enormous robotic tentacles, blowing themselves up and then noting down the results. Everything hummed, buzzed, boomed or crackled. It was a cave of treasures, all glittering and shining, all surrounded by a rolling cavalcade of flember-filled cables.

'This . . . is amazing,' he gasped, nudging Santoro.

'It's unusual.' Santoro nodded.

A small army of medic droids heaved and puffed,

struggling to carry Boja along behind. He was fast asleep now, his tongue lolloping so far out of his mouth it dragged along the floor with a loud SQUE-E-E-EAK.

At the sound of it, all the scientists stopped what they were doing. The explosions quietened. The smoke cleared. Now, instead, they stared at Boja. One of them, the tallest, skinniest scientist, wild curly hair spilling out from her head as if it were a bundle of stray thoughts, nervously poked his belly.

'What's he made from?' She grinned. 'Some sort of poly-flibbulate rollercore?'

'Umm, mostly bits of engine and cogglescrews.' Dev shrugged. 'A few whistlewires. Oh, and I think there's an inflated bilge sack in there too.'

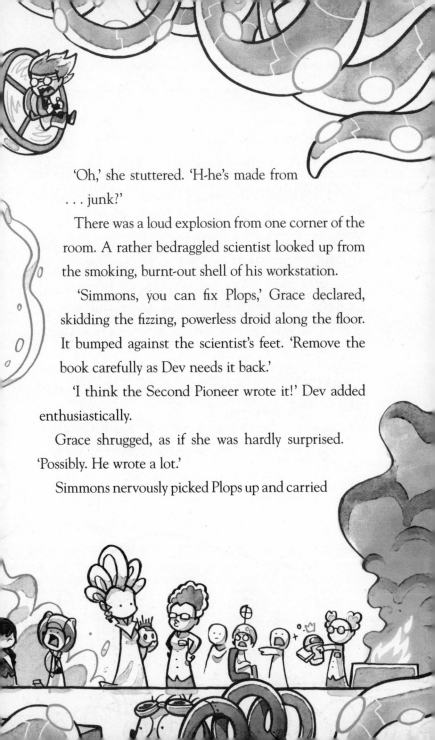

'Oh,' she stuttered. 'H-he's made from
. . . junk?'

There was a loud explosion from one corner of the
room. A rather bedraggled scientist looked up from
the smoking, burnt-out shell of his workstation.

'Simmons, you can fix Plops,' Grace declared,
skidding the fizzing, powerless droid along the floor.
It bumped against the scientist's feet. 'Remove the
book carefully as Dev needs it back.'

'I think the Second Pioneer wrote it!' Dev added
enthusiastically.

Grace shrugged, as if she was hardly surprised.
'Possibly. He wrote a lot.'

Simmons nervously picked Plops up and carried

him at arm's length over to his workstation.

'Everyone else,' Grace announced. 'You'll be fixing the bear.'

The scientists muttered excitedly, huddling around Boja and poking him with strange, bendy tools the like of which Dev had never seen before. Grace beckoned to the one with the wildest hair. 'Nerise,' she whispered. 'Boja needs a complete overhaul. He may be a robot but it's *flember* that powers him, and right now that flember is all out of sorts. I need you to rewire his circuits, check his flibbles, niggleswitch his limps, flomps and swipples, install a thirty-seven rerouter and tie it all up with a circuit-breaker.'

Nerise pushed her glasses up her nose. 'A . . . circuit-breaker?'

'I want Boja to be running at one hundred and fifty per cent,' Grace said. 'The very best Prime he can be.'

Nerise nodded, beckoning the medic droids as they carried Boja towards a large white table. The jostling woke Boja up. He giggled, sparkly clouds of flember spilling out of his nose as he was FLUMP-ed onto the table.

'BREAKFASCHT,' he gurgled, before promptly falling asleep again.

'Lock his legs,' Grace insisted, prompting a few of the

scientists to pull a set of rather large leather straps across Boja's wrists and ankles. 'We don't want him sparking up and whizzing across the room.'

'Are you sure about this?' Santoro whispered to Dev.

Dev wasn't sure at all. He could feel a bubbling panic rising inside him. 'Grace,' he started. 'I . . . I can fix Boja by myself. I built him after all. Just . . . just let me use some of your tools . . .'

A huge, domed screen appeared above Boja's snoring body. It flickered with all manner of readings: Boja's pulse, his breathing, his flember, every screw, bolt and bilious cord inside his body, each labelled and listed meticulously. Even a tiny lump of waffle, still wedged between his lung and his ribs, from when Dev had dropped a bit of his breakfast inside Boja's unfinished body.

Cables snaked down from above, circling around the bear. These weren't like the cables Dev had seen before, however. These cables were thin, black, recoiling just above Boja's belly, then firing thin smoky lines of coloured light into his fur.

'Boja is in the hands of the experts,' Grace said. 'Let them do their thing.'

Dev clutched his brother's hand tightly. They watched as the coloured lights danced across Boja's body, the domed screen tracking each and every movement inside him. Dials turned, channels rerouted, everything pulled out and then slotted back together at a slightly different angle. Dev's fears slowly started to fade away, replaced instead by an overwhelming awe at what was happening in front of him.

Boja was being rebuilt from the inside.

'We've the Third Pioneer to thank for all this,' Grace whispered, clutching the skull as she watched the scientists work. 'Iola Gray was her name. She worked with robotics. She designed the cables that carry the flember. She built the droids. She created the armour for our racers. She automated everything that serves us. Every piece of technology you see around you is because of her brilliance.'

There came a loud bang from behind them. Simmons, the scientist who had been working on Plops, had just been electrocuted. His hair all stood up on end. And he may have been slightly on fire. But to Dev's great relief he was holding the flember book in his hand.

'BEEP! Rule 052!' Plops suddenly declared. 'Only authorized Primes may – COCONUT – tamper with droids.'

'It . . . uh, it appears to have a slight glitch,' Simmons stammered, handing the book to Grace. 'Here's the book, though. It was wedged into Plops's main flember circuit.'

'Flember *circuit?*' Dev asked.

Grace pointed towards a small, square circuit on Plops' back. It had been broken, as the deep indent from the flember book would suggest, but still the sparkling light of flember crackled around inside it. 'Iola's finest achievement. All the droids have one.' She smiled. 'Oh, don't worry, the flember's safely concealed within strands of blackrock glass. Do you know blackrock? Most impenetrable material on the island – even flember can't pass through it. So *this* flember won't bring the droid to life or anything ridiculous like that. Instead, we send the flember whizzing round and round just fast enough to turn the flemberthyst blue, and once it's blue we know it's generating *power.*'

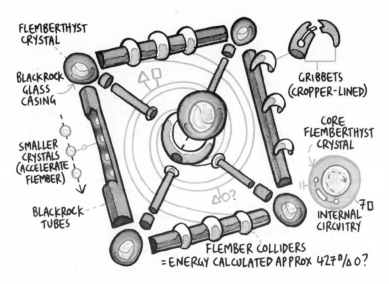

FLEMBERTHYST
CRYSTAL

BLACKROCK
GLASS
CASING

SMALLER
CRYSTALS
(ACCELERATE
FLEMBER)

BLACKROCK
TUBES

GRIBBETS
(CROPPER-LINED)

CORE
FLEMBERTHYST
CRYSTAL

INTERNAL
CIRCUITRY

FLEMBER COLLIDERS
= ENERGY CALCULATED APPROX 427°/△0?

She handed Dev the flember book, which he hurriedly stuffed safely into his backpack. 'We use this same technology throughout Prosperity. And when we're done with Boja, he'll be like one great big flember circuit. More efficient. More *powerful*.'

Dev smiled at the thought of Boja being well again, only for a loud clatter of alarms to make his heart jump. The screen above Boja was flashing. Streams of information spilled across it. Each and every scientist was panicking, frantically jabbing at Boja's huge, lumpen body.

'What's HAPPENING?' Dev shouted.

A set of large glass tanks either side of the table started to crackle and glow, great washes of flember swilling around inside them. 'He's overloading!' Nerise shouted, as she pulled out a cronklewrench and jabbed it into Boja's arm. Dev raced between them all, clambering on top of Boja's stomach and yanking the thin black cables away from his fur. 'I should never have let you touch him! I can fix him!' he shouted. 'Whatever's wrong, *I can fix him!*'

Suddenly a cable wrapped around Dev's stomach, hauling him away from the bear. He screamed and kicked, writhing to break free.

'Let him go!' Santoro yelled, drawing his sword, only

for another cable to tighten around his wrist. Within an instant he was pulled up too, off the floor, both Everdew brothers dragged away from Boja and flung through a large open door.

'I'm sorry,' Grace said, the skull glowing between her hands. 'But you're only making things worse.'

'BOJA!' Dev cried. He rushed to the door as it slammed shut. The hinges creaked and the cables locked into place, as each and every flemberthyst drained of light.

And Dev and Santoro were locked out.

17
Brothers

Soft, calming music played. Dev glanced around. He and Santoro had been thrown into what appeared to be a waiting room, decorated with comfy chairs, pot plants and a reception desk. Behind the desk hovered a nurse droid, already dented from its previous encounter with Boja.

'Welcome to The Lilac Rooms, wher—' it started, but Dev wasn't listening.

'I can get us out of here.' He hurriedly reached into his pocket and pulled out his key, then jammed it underneath the door's central orb. TWIST! Its thin strands of metal buckled between his fingers.

His heart sank.

He spun round, looking for something else he could use. The chair? The plant? The droid, maybe? He swung his bag from his shoulders to see what else he had with him.

'A map of the Spire,' he said, pulling out its contents. 'The deflated Sewer Ball, the flember book, and loads of squished-up cakes.'

He scrunched his face up in panic. 'There must be something I can invent out of all this. There MUST.'

'I think we may need to be a little more *forceful*,' Santoro said, drawing his oversized sword back, then swinging it hard against the door. It hit with a loud CLANG. 'I-i-i-it's h-h-harder tha-a-an I-I-I-I thought!' he stuttered, the sword still wobbling in his hands.

'We *have* to get through.' Dev's voice started to crack. 'We have to help Bo—' Suddenly his words disappeared completely. His legs started to tremble. And a sobbing, shaking Dev crumpled hopelessly against the door.

'It's OK, Dev.' Santoro's voice fell to a hush. He knelt down beside his brother and placed a hand upon his shoulder. 'Maybe . . . maybe all those weirdo scientists in there really *are* brilliant, and maybe they *can* fix Boja. Maybe they're going to make him even better than before!'

'But I know how he works!' Dev sobbed. 'I'm the one who put all his parts together. I tightened all his coggle-nuts. I aligned his fart sensors. I unlapsed his *eyeballs*, Santoro, and that's not an easy thing to do!' He drew his knees up under his chin. 'I should be fixing Boja. It should be ME.'

What followed was a long, long silence. Dev could only stare at his feet. His mind was whirring, frantically running through all the things he had to hand and trying to put them together into some brilliant new invention, some-thing that could get

them through the door and back to Boja. But, at least for the moment, a floppy rubber ball and some squashed cakes really weren't going to get him very far.

'We've sat like this before,' Santoro eventually said.

Dev sniffed and wiped a tear from his cheek. 'Wh . . . what do you mean?'

'You and me, locked on the wrong side of a door, while everyone's panicking on the other side of it. You might be too young to remember.'

The faintest of memories rippled through Dev's head. 'Dad,' he whispered.

'You DO remember.' Santoro nodded sadly. 'You were only one, two maybe. I wasn't much older. I sat beside you like this. You were upset, and I was trying to think of what to say to make you feel better, but I didn't quite know the words yet.'

He thought for a moment.

'I guess I still don't.'

'They took Dad indoors.' Clear shapes were starting to form in Dev's memory. 'Into the house. He was screaming and shouting – he was in *pain*.' He could feel a lump in his throat again. Tears wobbled in his eyes. 'Mum always said it was an accident. Something to do with the fields, the old machinery. But they wouldn't let us in to see him. They wouldn't open the door.'

Santoro nodded. 'All we could do was sit on the step and wait for him to come back out.'

Dev and Santoro both stared at each other. Neither of them wanted to finish the story.

'I never understood why they didn't just *fix* him,' Dev said. 'Even then. I remember thinking they're adults, adults fix things, so why can't they just . . . fix each other?'

'You can't fix everything.' Santoro sighed.

Dev shuffled onto his knees. He smushed the book, the floppy Sewer Ball and the squished cakes back inside his bag. 'I think I can, though,' he said. 'I've *always* thought I can.'

He rose to his feet, took a step back, and threw himself hard against the door. 'LET US IN!' he cried, before lunging at it again. 'I CAN FIX BOJA!'

Santoro watched his brother with a new-found admiration. Then he too stood up, drew out his sword and swung it again at the door. 'HEY!' Santoro shouted. 'MY BROTHER' – CLANG! – 'CAN HELP! LET HIM' – CLANG! – 'TRY!'

Suddenly the flemberthysts around the furthest edge of the door started to glow, bright sparkling flember hopping from one to the next. It unwrapped the locks, turned the hinges, glimmered up towards the central orb.

Dev and Santoro stood back as the door creaked open. And Dev saw Boja waving at them from his table.

18
The New Boja

Boja was sitting upright, his arms out in front of him. His wide, bulging eyes watched flember crackle along his fur, around his paws, dancing across his fingertips.

And he giggled.

'Boja?' Dev and Santoro raced through the Development Rooms. 'Boja, are you OK?'

Upon seeing Dev, Boja's smile widened. 'DEVVVV!' He beamed, just as Dev slammed into his side, wrapping his arms as far as they would stretch around the bear's big red belly. Dev breathed deeply of Boja's fur, flember sparkling up his nose.

The Prime scientists all looked frazzled, exhausted, their glasses skew-whiff and their hair, particularly

Nerise's, corkscrewed out in all manner of directions. She closed the screen she'd been working on, and unplugged the last cable from Boja's fur.

'He might be a bit confused at first,' she said.

Dev snapped round. 'What did you DO to him?'

'And WHY did you lock us out?' Santoro snarled.

'We were *fixing* him.' Grace stood beside Boja. She ran her fingers along his fur and watched, curiously, as his flember trailed around her fingertips. 'We *improved* him.'

'And what does that bit do?' Santoro pointed his sword towards something clamped over Boja's shoulders and onto his chest. It looked, to Dev, a bit like his own backpack. Boja's backpack, however, was made from gleaming metal. Thin lines of flember glowed along it, threading down to a central orb, which flickered and hummed with sparkly light.

Nerise coughed awkwardly. 'Uh . . . well, Boja was failing because his flember wasn't flowing around his body properly. Dev, you did very well making Boja how you did, but I don't think even you expected his insides to be put under so much *stress*.'

Dev thought back to when Boja first held the entire flember of a mountaintop, then rolled all the way down to the sea, then ate all the hibbicus and inadvertently exploded half of Darkwater, then sucked up all the flember from the mines, then—

'He . . . he's been through a lot,' he stammered.

Boja smiled a huge, delighted smile, then went back to staring at his fingers.

'Well, if we hadn't got to Boja when we did,' Nerise continued, 'he might have lost control of his own flember completely. We had to reroute it.' She tugged on the straps across Boja's shoulders. 'These clamps propel Boja's flember around his body in a loop, you see. And it all passes through this bit, in the middle—'

'The circuit-breaker,' Grace interrupted.

Nerise glanced at her nervously. 'Yeah, the . . . the circuit-breaker. Now Boja should finally be in control of his own flember. He can channel it wherever he needs it in his body, *whenever* he needs it.'

Dev looked up into Boja's eyes, still refusing to let go

of him. Although he was still angry at being locked out, his relief at seeing Boja had all but overcome him. 'How're you feeling?' he asked.

'WAFFFFFLES!!' Boja shouted, suddenly chomping down onto his own paws. 'YOWWWWW!' he then yelled, pulling his crumpled fingers from between his teeth and waggling them in the air.

'As I said, he might be a bit confused . . .' Nerise said.

Santoro snorted. 'He seems pretty normal to me.'

'Boja now runs on the same principle as Prosperity itself,' Grace said. 'Our city acts like one big flember circuit. Flember comes in, it gets carried all the way to the top of the Spire, the *Storm*, then we propel it out through the cables.'

She smiled proudly at Boja.

'And now your bear works in a similar way.'

'Thank you,' Dev said. 'Thank you all for fixing Boja. Thank you for keeping him alive.'

'Yeah, thanks, Santoro begrudgingly grumbled.

'FANKSCHHH.' Boja beamed, looking at the unchewed fingers on his other paw, and clearly wondering whether to try chewing them too.

'And the best thing is,' Nerise chipped in, 'with Boja's new circuitry, his capacity has been increased. He can hold more flember than ever before!'

Dev swung round to Grace, and let out an excited squeak. 'Does that mean—'

'It means Boja can now borrow a little of Prosperity's flember.' Grace smiled. 'But in return, there's something I was hoping you could all do for *us*.'

19
The Armoury

Dev and Santoro said their goodbyes and thank yous to all the scientists, then Boja did the same, albeit while chewing his fingers, before Grace and Plops led them back into the elevator and up to the next floor. As they walked out across the bridge, Dev in particular had a spring in his step. Boja was OK. Santoro was here. All they had to do was help Grace out with whatever she needed, then they could borrow some flember and they'd all be going home.

He could barely believe it.

'FIFTH FLOOR!' Plops rushed past him. 'Welcome to the – FIG ROLLS – Armoury! Please do not touch any of the – SLOPPY HAT – weapons.'

He stopped short of a set of huge, thick, ornate doors. Whatever secrets this floor held, they weren't for just anyone to see.

'Armoury?' Santoro's eyes lit up. 'Did you say *armoury*?' He quickened his pace towards the doors, tugging on their locked parts. 'Oh, Dev, finally we've found something here for ME.'

'Dev, would you?' Grace beckoned for Dev to open the doors.

Dev felt a little embarrassed. 'I, uh, I can't. I broke my key.'

A smile lingered on Grace's lips, as if she already knew. 'Maybe your little contraptions will only get you so far after all,' she said, stepping towards the doors and lifting the glowing skull. With a CLUNK CLANK CLONK, the hinges, rufflescrews and pipplecogs started to unlock from each other, and the doors opened with a loud CRE-E-E-EAK.

Santoro was first inside. He gazed up at the hanging armour, all the weapons he couldn't even begin to recognize. Knobbly things, sharp things, long things and wobbly things, all of them embedded with flemberthyst crystals. 'My sword's the only decent weapon in Eden,' he beamed, pulling what looked like a staff from the wall and swinging it around. 'But this stuff is next level.

What I could DO with weapons like these!'

'DO NOT TOUCH THE – CHICKEN BUMS – EQUIPMENT!' Plops demanded, whizzing around Santoro, its long metal arm desperately trying to grab the staff from his hands. But Santoro was too quick, too agile, chuckling as he danced around the droid.

'It's fine.' Grace smiled, leading Dev and Boja deeper inside. 'Let them try it, Plops. Let them try it all.'

Dev's eye caught a particularly shiny suit of armour hanging above him. He reached up and unhooked it, then hauled it down and slipped it over his shoulders. It looked bulky, but it felt amazingly light.

'What is this even made from?' he asked, lunging back and forth as he put the armour through its paces. 'I've never seen metal like this.'

'RMPH!' Boja huffed.

Dev turned round, then burst into laughter. The big red bear had pulled the helmet from one of the suits of armour and attempted to wedge it onto his head, but he had only managed to stuff one ear inside it. He wore gloves too, and a chest plate, but it had all been thoroughly split, stretched beyond all recognition.

'Boja, this isn't armour for you,' Dev fussed. 'You're too big for it!'

'Not too big.' Boja clung onto his helmet and tried to wedge it further down onto his ear.

'Boja, let me . . .' Dev reached up, only for the lights on his own armour to glow. He stepped back in surprise. Plink-plink-plink, they grew brighter, and brighter, all following the thin threads towards the centre of his chest.

'These *are* flemberthysts,' Dev gasped, as a tiredness started to come upon him. 'And they're being lit by MY flember. Ralto told me they were lights, just for show, but . . . but . . .' Suddenly the tiredness was gone. His every muscle started to twitch. The hairs across his skin started to bristle. His heart started to race. The flemberthysts flickered in sequence around his body, and as they did a wave of pure *exhilaration* washed over him.

'This . . . feels . . . INCREDIBLE!'

He lunged forwards, through the Armoury, knocking Plops into a rack of shields as he pelted out towards a circular boundary overlooking the Development Rooms. Then he hopped up onto the railing and jumped, not down, but across, clearing the wide gap and landing perfectly on the far side, before spinning around and jumping back.

'It's no WONDER Primes win all their races.' Dev

grinned wildly towards the rather stunned faces of Santoro and Boja. 'The armour isn't just being lit by my flember – it's being *powered* by it. The flember-thyst crystals send it racing around my body at speed like . . . like a big flember circuit! I feel so strong. I feel so fast. I feel . . . *supercharged*!'

Grace walked slowly around the railings. She remained as peacefully calm as ever. 'I knew you'd figure it out sooner or later,' she said. 'You're such a clever little boy.'

'Ohhh, Rails and Brianne would LOVE to see this.' Dev beamed. And then his face dropped. All his enthusiasm suddenly disappeared. 'But this . . . this isn't fair. The Lessers can't make armour like this for them-selves, as they don't have any flemberthysts!'

'True.' Grace smiled. 'And that will work to your advantage when you race against them.'

'WHAT?' Santoro yelled.

'WHAT?' Dev agreed. 'Why . . . why would I be racing?'

'Well, Prosperity has already given you so much.' Grace held a hand out towards Boja. 'We've shown you such wonders. We healed and improved your bear. And, as agreed, we'll be giving you some of our flember so you can heal your Eden Tree.'

Boja stood, helmet still wedged awkwardly onto his head.

'Surely it's not a lot to ask that in return you do something for Prosperity? That you run the third Pioneer Race on behalf of Prime?' Grace opened her arms out wide. 'Santoro and Boja too. All three of you, racing together. You'll be wearing our most advanced flember armour. And when you win, you'll be protecting this city's flember for its Prime citizens.'

'We're not running any race!' Santoro shouted, flinging his staff to the ground. 'Dev just wanted to borrow some flember, then we're going home. Your silly races have nothing to do with us!'

'And you already HAVE racers anyway! Esco, and . . . and Ralto, and the one who never says anything!' Dev protested.

Grace rolled her eyes. 'My beloved children are very

talented, but they won't win the third race,' she said.

'How can you *know* that?'

'I just . . . know,' Grace replied, a sly look in her eye. 'I—'

'Dev, we should go,' Santoro interrupted. 'Whatever she's doing here, why ever she's doing it, it's nothing to do with us.'

Dev scowled at Grace. 'This isn't right,' he said, slowly backing away from her. 'The Lessers deserve to share in Prosperity's flember. They deserve everything you already have. Your racers were only faster because of their armour. That's *cheating*.'

Grace let out a long, pained sigh. 'Oh, well, I *also* knew you would say all this.' She gripped the skull with both hands, as it glowed brighter between her fingers. 'Of course I did. I just hoped, perhaps, that I wouldn't have to do what happens next.'

At the other end of the Armoury Dev saw a long, shiny cable rise behind Boja like a whittlesnake. Before he could yell out a warning, the cable spun round the bear's ankle and tightened sharply. 'ROAAAAAOWWWW!' Boja yelled, as flember crackled across his body and then flew away from his fur, spinning out around him in great arcs of light. He clawed frantically, trying to pull it all back inside his body.

'What's HAPPENING to him?' Dev's own flember armour blazed and then he was in motion, leaping in great bounds towards Boja, only for another cable to whip out from beside him, sending him crashing into a rack of spears.

'Do you know what a *failsafe* is?' Grace said, as casually as if she was pouring a cup of tea. 'It's how we shut a machine down if it loses control. When we were upgrading Boja we gave him more control of his own flember, of course, but in granting him this extra power we had to make sure he wouldn't . . . misuse it.'

Boja howled, collapsing to the floor. Santoro rushed to help, only for another cable to whip him back down the long corridor and into a pile of discarded armour parts.

'The failsafe is a small addition concealed inside the circuit-breaker, then hardwired into Boja's entire nervous system,' Grace continued. 'Should he act against the interests of Prime it will clamp tightly around his flember and start squeezing it into a fine thread, before forcibly pulling it back into the Flember Stream. Quite a painful sensation, by the looks of it.'

'Please!' Dev shouted, clattering himself upright. 'Please make it stop!'

'Flember must be *controlled* if we are to maintain a civilized society!' Grace said firmly, thick, glowing cables writhing around her like the waves of the sea. 'Your bear, your *machine*, has been granted such gifts by Prosperity, and I'll not have him use those gifts against us.'

'We'll race!' Dev yelled. 'We'll race for you. Just let him go!'

Grace watched him for a moment. Then the skull's

eyes started to dim. The cable let go of Boja's ankle. His breaths became calmer, shallower. Flember rippled back inside his fur.

His chest heaved.

His eyes flickered.

And he slumped down onto his bottom.

Dev threw himself against Boja's gently heaving belly. 'I'm so sorry,' he sobbed. 'I'm so sorry I ever let Grace fix you!'

Boja gurgled, his eyes still spinning, his golden heart DOOMPF-DOOMPF-DOOMPF-ing wildly inside his chest.

'Brckfschth?' he mumbled hopefully.

'Breakfast,' Dev winced. 'Soon. Somehow.'

'Win the race for me,' Grace smirked. 'Win the race and you can have all the flember and breakfast you can carry. Then, and only then, you can all go home.'

20
Three New Racers

The evening skies above Prosperity twinkled with stars, but none of them shone more beautifully than the Spire itself. The cables that wrapped around it all pulsed with bright, sparkling flember, lighting it up like a web of dew-laden silk.

Dev's mind, however, was on other things. He walked out across the concourse, towards the statue in its centre. He fiddled nervously with his flember armour, readjusting the straps, then checking the flemberthysts wired along them. 'What am I even doing here?' he muttered, his breath curling out in front of him. 'We can't race against Brianne. But we can't afford to *lose* either. Think, Dev, think! Fix this!!'

CLANK! CLANK! CLANK! Santoro walked along behind him. He wore flember armour of his own. His was larger, spikier, the boots heavier, the gauntlets chunkier. His sword was his own, however, dragging along the ground and leaving sparks in its wake.

'She was never going to give you any flember,' Santoro growled. 'Grace, I mean, and that weird old skull of hers. She's been playing us all along.'

'But *why*? And how does she know so much about us?' Dev turned to look up at the third-floor balcony. A crowd of Primes stared back down at him, whispering nervously between themselves. Grace stood in front of them all, the skull's glow ebbing gently against her chest.

'Why would she risk the third race on US?'

There came a loud CLOMP-CLOMP-CLOMP along the concourse. Boja was a little too big for anything in the Armoury, but he had still squeezed into a few more pieces of armour just for the fun of it. He did, however, look a little wobbly. Dev was about to ask him how he was feeling when Boja's feet suddenly tripped over each other, and instantly the bear crashed down onto his face.

'AM OK!' Boja mumbled, peeling off all the crumpled bits of armour. 'Squashed my nose.'

The Primes watching from the balcony all groaned and put their heads in their hands. Grace, however,

seemed as calm as ever. She sailed towards the front railings and held the skull of Cervantes Escobar up high so everyone could see it.

And then the skull glowed brighter.

A distant cheer rumbled from over the boundary. As before, the buildings started to rise from behind it, great plumes of dust catching the low light and shrouding the gardens in cloud. A large crowd of Lessers, yelling and punching the air, roaring in anticipation, rode upon the rooftops.

As three figures stepped through.

Brianne led from the front. She appeared to have upgraded her armour even more since the second race. It was bigger, now. Bulkier. The exploded rocket-pack had been replaced with a newer, larger version. She heaved and hissed as she moved, striding across the rooftops and then slamming noisily down onto the racetrack. The other two racers, Pipo and Dollop, both similarly beefed up, leapt down behind her. Then, as before, the racetrack itself started to split apart. Whole sections carried the three Lesser racers high across the gardens, Brianne's growling, determined face flashing across the screens as they leapt purposefully down onto the concourse.

Then Brianne saw Dev.

And her expression fell into one of utter disbelief.

'You're . . . you're racing *against* us?' she cried.

'HI, BREE-YAN!' Boja waved cheerfully.

'It . . . it's not what you think,' Dev whispered. 'We *have* to.'

Brianne rolled her eyes, flexed her huge metal arms and slammed a heavy grille down across the front of

her helmet. 'Fine, whatever.' She shrugged, taking her position on the other side of the statue. 'I'm still going to win this race. I'll go through all three of you if I have to!'

'GOOD PEOPLE OF PROSPERITY.' Grace's face appeared on the screens. The crowds hushed. 'Here we are, at our final Pioneer Race of the day. A race none of us have had to run before.' She cast a glance to Esco, Ralto and Sienna, all grumpily huddled at the far end of the balcony. 'But like everyone, we are all at the mercy of whatever fate might hold in store for us.'

The screens flashed back onto Brianne. 'As you will already be aware,' Grace continued, 'this morning a *Lesser* won the first race, and as a result, claimed the compass.'

Brianne proudly placed a hand over the compass welded onto her chest. The crowds beyond the boundary cheered wildly.

'Then, in the second race, our magnificent Prime racer claimed the whitedrop.' Grace gestured to Sienna. She too had the whitedrop embedded into the front of her armour, but there was no delight in her face, no pride. Only a long, heavy, sulky expression.

'So it is,' Grace continued, 'that by our own fair rules, both Prime and Lesser must race *one more time* to decide an outright winner, to determine how Prosperity's flember will be shared for the rest of the year!'

The Lessers along the outskirts cheered loud enough for the noise to rattle through Dev's armour. The Lesser racers too whooped and hollered, clanging their fists against their chests. Each clang sank Dev's stomach deeper, and deeper, down inside him.

Grace held the glowing skull high until the crowds had settled down. 'As the First Pioneer, I designed Prosperity,' she proudly recited. 'The Second Pioneer filled it with flember. But the *Third* Pioneer . . .'

The concourse started to rumble. The rumble then became a CRA-A-A-ACK, as the space before Dev's feet sank down to form a wide, deep bowl around the statue, leaving it some height above where the ground once was.

'. . . the Third Pioneer turned that flember into *POWER.*'

Dev stared at the statue standing tall inside the bowl. It was a woman. Tall, thin, gaunt. She had a pointed nose, sharp, beady eyes, and a long chin. Her hair was straggly, unkempt. Her back straight. She wore robes of a sort, ruffled along her arms and dragged down across her feet. And there, in her outstretched hands, she held the tool that looked like a fizzleswitch, or a clonkdriver. But Grace had called it something else. What was it she said?

'The *Cronklewrench*,' Santoro growled. 'I suppose that's what we're supposed to grab, is it?'

'Racers may use whatever means necessary to reach the Cronklewrench,' Grace declared. 'But whoever wins it must do so by sheer strength of character. As such, the rules decree that flying will NOT be permitted in this race.'

The Lesser crowd let out a loud AWWW. Brianne's new rocket-pack let out a disgruntled puff of smoke.

'Leap all you will,' Grace continued. 'Jump high. But if I decide that your armour actually helps you *fly* . . .'

Thick, bulging cables rose from beneath the concourse. They curled around each other as they arched high into the night sky, then pointed down towards the statue. Santoro instinctively drew his sword against them as they quivered closer, and closer, as if waiting to strike.

'. . . then the cables will bring you back down to the ground.' Grace grinned.

'However this race goes,' Dev's voice trembled, 'Grace isn't going to let the Lessers win. The Primes can't afford to lose their flember.'

'Well, if you have any ingenious ideas for how we might get out of this, now's the time to mention them!' Santoro whispered.

Dev glanced to the Primes on the balcony, to the Lessers on the boundary. He caught sight of Brianne, her metal fingers clenching as she readied herself for what was to come. And he saw Boja, swaying back and forth. His tongue was drooping slightly out of his mouth. His eyes were drifting off in different directions.

And Dev felt a grim inevitability about what was about to happen.

'I don't think there is any way out,' he gulped, as a loud HON-N-N-N-N-NKK echoed across Prosperity. 'I think we have to race.'

21
The Race for the Cronklewrench

The Lesser racers all charged for the statue. It was not a graceful scene. The curved walls of the bowl were steeper than they looked, dragging them all down as they slipped and crumpled over each other.

From the other side Santoro was just as quick. 'Let's get this over with,' he yelled, before skidding down inside the bowl. Dev rushed behind, holding his footing for as long as he could, but soon he too was rolling head over heels, flattening out just in time to see a giggling, swaying Boja sliding merrily down towards him.

'Look out!' Dev shouted. 'LOOK OU—'

Boja couldn't have stopped if he'd tried. He slammed Dev into the stone column below the statue, squishing his face into a big cushion of butt fur. All the sounds and commotion muffled in Dev's ears. For a moment, just a moment, everything felt calm.

'SOH-RRY!' Boja exclaimed, leaning away so Dev could breathe again. The noise rushed back in. Dev's eyes uncrossed to see cables swinging wildly around above him, Lesser racers grabbed by their ankles as they were picked up and then slammed down across the concourse.

'NO FLYING!' Grace's voice boomed out from the screens.

'We weren't!' Pipo cried, crawling back towards the bowl.

Dev staggered onto his feet, staring down at the wildly flickering lights of his own armour. Something was wrong. Boja's ample bottom had cracked some of the flemberthyst crystals. Dev could feel his flember stuttering, jolting, straining to pass between them.

'Shame,' Brianne growled in his ear, before pushing Dev out of the way and flinging herself at the foot of the statue. Her armour huffed and puffed as she started to climb, only for a cable to blindside her, sending her tumbling into Boja's open arms.

'COOOEEE!' Boja grinned goofily.

'You see who you're fighting for?' Brianne growled. 'Grace is CHEATING. She's using the cables to keep us back until one of YOU gets up there.'

Suddenly another cable wrapped around Boja's ankle, causing him to ROARRRRR out in pain. His flember spun out in a bright display of lights, the failsafe whirring noisily upon his chest. He dropped Brianne, barely able to stay on his feet.

'Boja!' Dev scrambled to get to him. Santoro, despite being within a sword's tip of the cronklewrench, threw himself back down to help.

'The flemberthysts!' Dev shouted. 'Crack the flemberthysts in the cable!'

Santoro drew his sword and swung it towards Boja's ankle. With a loud CRA-A-A-ACK it carved through one of the cable's flemberthysts. A sparkling puff of flember wisped out before sinking back down inside and disappearing into the next flemberthyst along. But now Dev could see inside the cable itself. He could see the straining pulleys, the insulated tubes, all its inner workings. 'They're mechanical.' He gasped. 'The cables are powered by flember, but they move like *robots*.'

He stared up at Grace, at the glowing skull in her

CONTRAPTION: Flemberthyst Cable
(Dev's best guess)

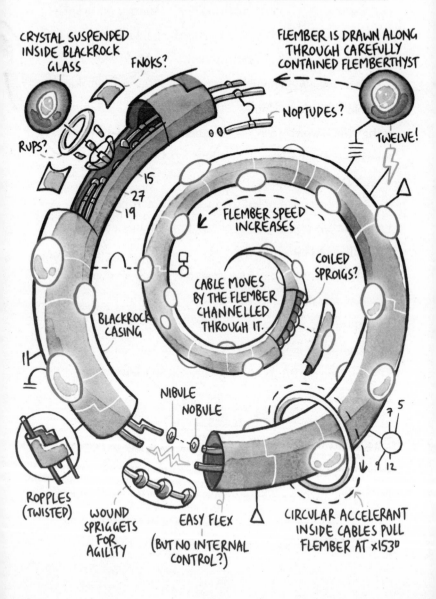

CRYSTAL SUSPENDED INSIDE BLACKROCK GLASS

FNOKS?

RUPS?

FLEMBER IS DRAWN ALONG THROUGH CAREFULLY CONTAINED FLEMBERTHYST

NOPTUDES?

TWELVE!

15
27
19

FLEMBER SPEED INCREASES

COILED SPROIGS?

CABLE MOVES BY THE FLEMBER CHANNELLED THROUGH IT.

BLACKROCK CASING

NIBULE
NOBULE

ROPPLES (TWISTED)

WOUND SPRIGGETS FOR AGILITY

EASY FLEX (BUT NO INTERNAL CONTROL?)

7   5

9   12

CIRCULAR ACCELERANT INSIDE CABLES PULL FLEMBER AT ×153⁰

hands. 'And she's holding the remote control.'

'YOWWWWWW!' Boja yelped even louder.

'Can you *fix* them?' Santoro shouted, slamming his sword into another flemberthyst. 'Break them, rewire them, do something to stop them?'

'I . . . I don't know,' Dev stammered. 'Their technology is way beyond anything I've ever—'

'GR-O-O-O-O-O-ORAGHHHH!' Boja suddenly boomed, as more cables slapped around his legs, his wrists, lifting his whole body up from the ground. His flember whirled around his body like a tornado.

'You race for Prime,' Grace's stern voice echoed across Prosperity.

'Well, *I* don't.' Brianne cried, leaping through the mass of cables. One buckled, then whipped around to strike her. With lightning-fast reactions she swung a fist to her own rocket-pack and blasted the cable with flame. The force sent her rocketing away from Boja, and crumpling into Dev.

'I get it,' she said, 'I get why you're all doing this now. Grace is controlling *everything*.'

Then she froze. Her face went deathly pale. Dev turned to see what she was looking at, his blood running cold as he saw a number of cables rearing up around them like snakes.

'We'll protect Boja,' Dev spoke under his breath. 'Brianne, you need to get the Cronklewrench and finish this!'

Before he'd even finished his sentence, Brianne had bolted, speeding not up the statue, but around the bowl, leading the swarm of cables after her. Once she'd completed a lap she leapt onto the thickest of them, escaping their tips only by running along their trunks. Up she climbed, higher around the column, huffing and puffing as she clanked her way closer and closer to the cronklewrench.

Suddenly the cables overtook her. They slithered up in front of the statue and quivered, ready to strike. 'DEV?' Brianne backed away. 'ANY IDEAS?'

'I . . . I don't know,' Dev stammered, still tugging at the cables round Boja's ankles. Then, without a sound, the light faded from between his hands. The flemberthysts dulled, their flember draining along the cables as they slumped, lifeless from beneath Brianne's feet. She had only seconds left to grab the Cronklewrench before she'd slip down and sink into the squirming mass of cables.

Dev looked up at Boja. The bear was buzzing with flember. 'Cheated.' Boja beamed, flember sparkling out from between his teeth, his nose, his ears, his whole body rigid as if he was holding in the most almighty fart.

'*You're* being the circuit-breaker,' Dev gasped. 'They tapped you into the Flember Stream, so now you can block it from *reaching the cables.*'

'That's *incredible!*' Santoro gazed.

'HURTS!' Boja suddenly winced, as the huge, thunderous fart he'd been holding in suddenly blasted out from between his buttocks. As it did all the flember he'd been blocking rushed back through the cables, sending them whipping around Brianne and lifting her high away from the statue.

But she didn't care.

She was holding the Cronklewrench.

'We won!' she shrieked, barely able to believe it. 'We won the race! Two out of three! Prosperity's flember is OURS!'

22
A Rough Justice

Unsurprisingly the Prime crowd were less than excited about the outcome of the third Pioneer Race. They stared down from the viewing platform, aghast, hardly able to believe what had just happened. Grace, however, was not amongst them. She was already riding the elevator down through the Flember Stream, emerging on the ground floor with Plops and a cluster of police droids hovering alongside. Brianne was first to spot them. She hung upside down from her cable, thrusting the Cronklewrench out for all to see. 'Maybe the Primes are no better than the Lessers after all!' she laughed.

'BEEP!' Plops barked. 'Third Pioneer Race – FUSCHLENUTS – is declared void!'

'WHAT?!'

The cable dropped Brianne. She landed with a loud CRASH onto the concourse.

'In conspiring with our Prime guests,' Grace announced, 'Dev, Santoro, and the bear' – the screens flashed to Boja. Boja, still a little frazzled by what had just happened, managed a weak grin and a wave – 'the Lessers have proven themselves untrustworthy, and undeserving of Prosperity's flember.'

With a glow of the skull, a cable whipped the Cronklewrench out of Brianne's hands and passed it over to Grace. 'Furthermore, this will be the last of the Pioneer Races, not just this year, but for good. We generously tried to offer all citizens a chance to be equal, but it appears our trust was misplaced!'

The Prime crowd on the third floor started clapping politely, but it was soon drowned out by a thunderous sound of booing from the boundary. It would have grown louder too, were the buildings of the outskirts not already lowering out of sight. Soon all sign of dissent was conveniently out of view, and the Primes need not worry about it any more.

As the bowl started to flatten out again, Dev found himself being rolled back onto the concourse. He stood, then started staggering towards Grace. 'Brianne didn't cheat,' he shouted. 'She played by your rules and she beat you! If anyone's been cheating it's YOU.'

'Oh, Dev,' Grace whispered, the skull glowing between her hands. 'The rules don't apply to *me*.'

'HEY! GET OFF THEM!' Brianne suddenly yelped, as cables snared the other two Lesser racers, lifting their battered and exhausted bodies up high above the concourse. They were passed from cable to cable, out across the gardens and back towards the outskirts. More cables came for Brianne as she was lifted, kicking and screaming, directly over Dev's head, towards the outskirts where the boundary and the outer concrete wall converged so close, there was only a few metres between them.

And there she was held, dangling over the Wildening.

'Wh . . . what are you doing with her?' Dev demanded,
a sickening dread swirling around inside his belly.

'We cannot allow our rules to be undermined.' Grace
glided towards the edge of the concourse. 'This particular Lesser is not welcome in our city any more.'

'You can't throw her out there!' Santoro yelled. 'We've
been in the Wildening! It's like being in a nightmare!'

'Protocol must be – CHEESE DIPS – followed!' Plops
repeated, as the cables swung Brianne high above the

treetops. All the anger, all the determination from before had drained from her face. Now she looked small. Terrified.

'Please,' she shouted. 'I'm sorry. Just let me go *home*.'

'You can't do this,' Dev shouted. 'You CAN'T.'

Grace stared at the girl hanging high above the Wildening.

'Nothing will stand in the way of civilization,' she whispered. 'Nothing will stop the will of Cervantes Escobar.'

The cables suddenly loosened around Brianne.

And she dropped into the darkness like a rock into a lake.

Dev was quick to react. What remained of his flember armour lit up as he raced past Grace, past the line of

flashing police droids. 'If this is what Primes are like, then I'd rather be *Lesser*.' He scowled, leaping onto the cable and then out over the gardens racing towards its narrowest end.

And there, his nerves finally caught up with him.

He wobbled precariously over the Wildening. His heart pounded loudly in his chest.

'I COME TOO!' Boja suddenly charged, scattering a few police droids off the edge of the concourse as he jumped onto the cable. He landed with such a belly-flopping THUMP! it flicked the end of the cable up, propelling Dev into the darkening skies with a yelp. Boja scrambled to his feet, panicked, rushing to catch Dev as he dropped. But Dev was already too far out. All Boja could do was throw himself out after him, followed by the reassuring shape of Santoro close behind.

'This place is messed up,' Santoro panted, leaping out into the darkness as all three of them plummeted away from the Spire.

And down, into the Wildening.

23
The Wildening

Dev knelt in the cold, wet grass. He'd scraped down the bark of a spindletree and it showed. His face was whipped, his armour even more broken than before, its flember-thysts flashing and ebbing as they struggled to carry his flember from one end of his body to the other.

It took him a moment to remember where he was, but when he did all the colour drained from his cheeks.

'The Wildening,' he gasped, staring out into the darkness. Everything moved in the breeze. The plants, the bushes, the leaves of the trees – all of it swayed around him. Shadows crept closer. Something squawked. Something rustled. He scrambled back against Prosperity's outer wall and desperately tried to catch his breath.

'You didn't have to come out here.' Brianne coughed, she was upside down in a bobbleberry bush. Her armour looked pretty battered too. A thin trail of smoke whistled out from one of her canisters.

'No one should be in the Wildening on their own,' Dev replied, as he helped her roll upright again.

'I think we can all agree on that.' Santoro climbed down the spikes of a spindletree. Once on the ground he readjusted his flember armour, lifted his sword and pointed it out towards the shadows. 'Both of you, keep behind me. Whatever's out there, it's going to be—'

'COOOEEEE!' Boja suddenly yelled. They all looked up to see the big red bear wedged tightly between two thick tree branches, his arms left hanging towards the ground.

'Boja, can you get down?' Dev shouted.

Boja clenched his teeth and strained, waggling his legs as he tried to shake himself loose. Something did loosen. A billowing, bubbling fart, spilling out from between his buttocks.

He giggled.

'SHHH!' Santoro hissed, swinging his sword back towards the shadows. Dev could hear it too. A low, ominous growl coming out from between the trees. He peered into the gloom, only for a sharp pain to suddenly shoot through the scratches on his arm. His legs wobbled from beneath him.

He started to feel strange.

He started to feel woozy.

'THERE!' Santoro pointed his sword into the darkness. Something was moving. It crept slowly, carefully, its black skin glistening like oil. One long paw slid out in front of the other. Its rocky spine undulated. Its sharp teeth snarled.

Its red eyes glowed.

'The dark wolf,' Dev stammered, struggling to keep focus. 'Santoro, I've seen this thing before, but there . . . there were two of them!'

As if summoned, the second dark wolf flanked them from the other side; growling, snarling. Santoro swung his sword between them both, backing towards Dev and Brianne as he held his guard.

The pain in Dev's arm throbbed harder. Everything around him blurred. All the sounds – the desperate, frantic voices – it all became distorted noise in his ears. Even the touch of Brianne's hand upon his shoulder faded away.

'DEV!' Santoro shouted, snapping Dev back onto the damp grass, into the cold, fresh air. Dev barely had time to open his eyes again before the first wolf leapt towards them. Its teeth clanged either side of Santoro's blade. The sheer force pushed him backwards, as its snout bunched up into a furious snarl.

'It's too strong!' Santoro grimaced, his

flember armour flickering. 'I can't hold it back!'

'BOJA!' Dev yelled up into the trees. 'Boja, we need you!'

High up in the trees Boja waggled his legs. He strained and farted, farted and strained, the sparkling glow of flember crackling all across his body. It blazed behind his eyes, spilling out through his nostrils, pulling every strand of fur on end as he roared, and he roared, and he roared so loud the tree itself started to shake. FWOOM! Sparks sputtered out from his feet just as they had back in Prosperity, threading around his ankles like boots made of flember, blasting him down through the branches.

And throwing him upon the first dark wolf.

The wolf YELPED as Boja's not inconsiderable bottom crumpled it underneath. The second wolf didn't hesitate. It lunged towards the bear, teeth bared, eyes blazing. Boja lifted his paw back to swing a punch. As he did, a clear line of flember started to trace along his fur, spiralling around his fist, around his knuckles, drawing out the shape of a huge, glowing gauntlet. It hit the dark wolf square in the face, rocketing it not just up through the trees, but far, far into the night sky.

Dev, Santoro and Brianne all stared at Boja in amazement.

Boja smiled proudly.

Then he stood, allowing the crumpled remains of the first wolf to clamber out of his butt-crater. It limped back into the darkness, whimpering all the way like a poodlepig.

'Your bear.' Brianne stared at Boja in disbelief. 'He . . . he's so *powerful*!'

Dev patted Boja's flember back down inside his fur. 'The Prime scientists said they gave him more control of his flember. Maybe this is what they meant!'

'Guhhhh,' Boja added. His eyes were starting to close, a goofy, sleepy grin spreading across his face as he slumped back down onto his bum.

'Oh no, you can't sleep yet,' Santoro insisted, sheathing his well-chewed sword and readjusting his ruffled hair. 'Not while we're all stuck out here.'

'We can follow the outer wall!' Brianne declared. 'It'll lead us round towards the outskirts until we can climb back in. We'll be safe there – the cables can't reach us. That creepy old skull can't reach us.'

'Sounds good to me.' Dev rubbed the scratches on his arm, and sighed with relief. 'Anything to get us out of the Wildening.'

24
The Second Foundry

'It's inconceivable!' Rails cried, pacing around inside the Foundry. 'Inhuman! Throwing you out into the Wildening like that, it's . . . it's . . .'

'It was a fix.' Brianne sighed. The large open fire crackled in front of her, its light wobbling across the floor. 'They were never going to let us win the races. I was stupid to think they would.'

'Every Lesser was ready to come after you,' Rails said. 'Every single one of us. We'd only just stacked the ladders against the walls when we saw you climbing over the top.'

'Thank you.' Brianne sipped on a mug of tea. 'I'm just lucky I had Dev, Santoro and Boja with me.'

'Cakes!' Dev suddenly remembered. 'I took cakes from

the Primes!' He slipped off his backpack and opened it up to reveal what may, once, have been cakes from the Prime dining tables, but had long since become a goop of sludgy crumbs. He stared at the goop for a little while. 'I'm sorry,' he finally sighed.

'It's fine, we still have gritcake.' Brianne pulled a slice of bumpy, grey cake from the plate in front of her and offered it to Dev. He didn't take it. Boja did, however, then topped it with a pawful of sludgy crumbs from the ground.

'No, I don't mean the cakes,' Dev said as Boja chomped loudly beside him. 'I mean, I'm sorry we fought against you in the race. Grace found a way to hurt Boja, to *really* hurt him, and she said she'd do it again if we didn't compete against you.'

Santoro grunted from inside the open doorway. 'I never trusted Grace,' he said, busily trying to grind the deep bite marks from the blade of his sword. 'There's something really weird about her. Like, when Boja smashed up half her library, destroyed her precious statue, she wasn't angry about it at all!'

'She knows so much about us, ' Dev muttered. 'She knows everything we're going to do before we've even had the chance to do it. She probably even put us in the Third Pioneer Race because she knew we'd help Brianne, because then she'd have a reason to—'

Dev and Santoro both gasped.

'Throw us out of Prosperity TOO!' they both exclaimed.

'Well I'm sorry too,' Brianne interrupted. 'Because of all this you've lost your best chance of reaching the Flember Stream.'

Dev scraped the rest of the sludgy goop out of his backpack and lifted out the flember book. 'There are other places on the map,' he said. 'We can keep looking . . .'

'You shouldn't *have* to keep looking.' Brianne shrugged the blanket from her shoulders and got to her feet. 'It's all there, inside the boundary. Access to all the flember they, us AND you, could ever need! But here we are, back where we were before the races, no flember, no nothing. It's not fair!'

She picked up her discarded armour, SHOOF-ing a leg inside it. 'Well, I'm not just going to sit around here moaning about it. I'm going to find a way back inside

Prosperity.' CLANG. She locked the chest plate into position. 'I'm going to find Grace.' CLUNCH, the metal arms, the shoulder boosters. 'And I'm going to grab that stupid glowing skull right out of her hands.'

She held a metal hand down towards Dev. 'And then I'm going to share Prosperity's flember with everyone, *especially* you and Boja.'

A section of her shoulder armour fell off, clanging against the ground.

'I think . . . we might need to work on your armour first.' Dev smiled, sliding the flember book back inside his backpack.

Suddenly a wailing siren sounded from the streets outside. Rails leapt to his feet, pouring the last of the tea into the hissing fire. 'Police droids,' he whispered, clicking his fingers at Santoro to close the door. 'Quickly, shut it all down!'

Brianne ran to the large dials on the wall, spinning them around until the fire calmed into a tiny flame. Dev then flipped the tea cauldron upside down upon it, casting the Foundry into absolute darkness.

They all held their breath.

The red lights of a police droid flashed beneath the door. It stopped, as if it were listening. Then it carried on, its lights faded and the siren echoed away down the street.

'I bet Grace sent it out here looking for us,' Santoro grumbled. 'Somehow she must know we got out of the Wildening?'

'Oh, she *knows*,' Dev said. 'She knows everything we do. I don't know *how* she knows, but she just does.'

The siren wailed again from outside, so loud it made Dev's heart jump. This time the police droid wasn't taking any chances. It THUMPED against the door. THUMP. THUMP. Then THUMP, the door hinges buckled, and suddenly the droid was through.

Boja was nearest. He grabbed the droid and tried to muffle its sirens inside his furry arms, only for it to release a huge bolt of electricity in defence. Boja's eyes spun round in their sockets, his teeth chattering as he rattled across the floor like a wind-up toy.

'H-B-B-B-B-B-B!' he burbled.

'If it's anything like Plops it'll have a flember circuit!' Dev yelled, scrambling out of Boja's way. 'If we can just remove it, we could—'

There came a loud BEEE-WOOO.

The electricity faded.

Santoro stood, sword outstretched, its blade reaching between Boja's arms and impaling the droid's flember circuit with pinpoint accuracy. Then, with a flick, he wrenched it out, handing it to Dev like a piece of meat on a skewer.

'This thing?' he asked.

'Thanks!' Dev beamed, carefully plucking the circuit

from Santoro's sword and holding it up towards the moonlight. It glowed, and it crackled, and it hummed. 'And there's still flember in here,' he smiled. 'You didn't break the flemberthyst.'

Then, as sure as anything, an idea started to bubble away inside Dev's brain.

'We need to stay a little bit longer.' He grinned. 'Because I think I can help Brianne get the glowing skull.'

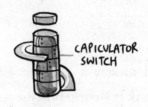

CAPICULATOR
SWITCH

25
The Flember Armour

Brianne eyed Dev's plans.

'What's a capiculator switch?'

'It's like a roppleflop.' Dev beamed. 'Only it leans slightly more to the left.'

'What's a roppleflop?' Rails whispered to Santoro. Santoro shrugged.

'We'll have to make a roppleflop from scratch,' Dev said, studying Brianne's armour. 'And we'll need to rejig what you're wearing, take the best bits. We're going to build something entirely new. And we're going to make it work with *this*.'

He wrenched the flemberthyst crystal out from the police droid's flember circuit, and plonked it down onto

INVENTION 508: Flember Armour
(Dev's version)

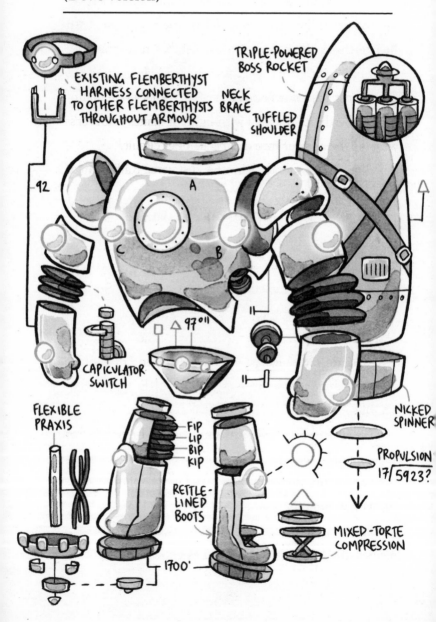

the middle of his plans.

'The reason the Prime racers always had such an advantage is because they filled their armour with flemberthysts. It sent their own flember racing around their bodies. It gave them a *supercharge*.' He clanged his fist against his own broken armour, as its few remaining flemberthysts crackled with light. 'It makes whoever's wearing the armour into one *big* flember circuit.'

More sirens sounded in the distance. Rails stared nervously at Brianne.

'So we stick a flemberthyst to my armour,' Brianne said, raising an eyebrow. 'It'll give me a little bit of charge. But the Prime armour was *covered* in flemberthysts. Just one of them won't carry me all the way into the Spire.'

'Oh, there are plenty more flemberthysts we can use.' Dev smiled, stepping over the remains of the police droid and leaning his head out through the open door. 'HEY, DROIDS!' he suddenly shouted. 'WE'RE IN HERE! COME AND GET US!'

'What are you DOING?' Rails clamped a hand over Dev's mouth and dragged him back inside. 'You'll bring ALL the police droids to the Foundry!'

'Mmpff mmphsch schmph.' Dev nodded.

Sirens wailed down the street. Red lights flashed against the buildings. The few Lessers who had peered out to see what was going on all suddenly ducked back inside their houses. Santoro, however, quickly realized what his brother was up to.

And Dev saw an admiring smile poke into his cheek.

'Ohhhh, I get it,' Rails chuckled in appreciation, as he and Santoro ran to one side of the open doorway, pointing Boja to the other.

'You're not going to have long, Dev,' Santoro warned.

'We won't need long.' Dev grinned, cracking his fingers.

The first police droid came screeching inside. Boja was swift to grab it, receiving an almighty electrical shock for his trouble while Santoro pierced the droid's flember circuit with his sword. He flung it over to Dev. Another droid swept in only to be headlocked by Rails, the next hugged by Boja, each of the droids relieved of their flember circuits as they electrified their captors.

Dev set to work with a fizzing excitement in his belly. He started by pulling out the flemberthysts and

then clamping them to Brianne's armour, then wiring them together with blackrock thread. Some pieces he needed to swap out – an arm here, a leg there, a triple-powered boss rocket round the back – swiftly tweaking and clanging and tightening as he went.

'They're still coming!' Santoro shouted over what sounded like a hundred sirens outside. A mound of power-less, smoking droids blocked the doorway. In the flashing red lights Boja's fur looked utterly frazzled. Santoro and Rails too were starting to look exhausted.

'It's OK, we're DONE!' Dev cheered.

Brianne's armour looked a mess, a disjointed mish-mash of metal and wires, all of them bundled together with one large, makeshift flember circuit running across her body.

'Are you ready?' Dev grinned.

'Plug me in!' Brianne replied, an excited twin-kle in her eyes. Dev gripped the loose wires along her arm, knotted them together and plugged them directly into her harness. Instantly a line of glowing, sparkling flember drifted out, swirling around each flemberthyst before passing on towards the next.

Her armour slowly heaved, as if it was waking from a thousand years sleep.

'I feel . . .' Brianne gasped. 'I feel . . . *tired*.'

'Your flember's being pulled out of your body.' Dev helped steady her. 'You might feel tired at first, but—'

Suddenly something in Brianne changed. Her cheeks flushed red, her body stiffened. All across her armour the flemberthysts flickered in sequence.

'ROARRRR!' she boomed, stamping her foot down hard, only to leave a deep footprint in the ground. 'Dev, this feels AMAZING!'

'YO, THAT'S GREAT AND ALL!' Rails shouted from the doorway, a police droid under each arm. 'BUT WE CAN'T STAY HERE!'

As he spoke a swarm of police droids barged through the bodies of their fallen companions, sending a sea of electrified robot parts spilling through the Foundry. The sirens were deafening. The lights blinding.

'GO!' Rails insisted.

Before Dev knew what was happening, Brianne had wrapped a chain around his arm. 'This is how we get out in emergencies.' She winked, yanking the chain down hard as it dragged Dev off the ground and up into the rafters.

Up, towards the cool night sky above.

Once at the very top of the Foundry, Dev's feet found a teetering succession of wooden platforms. He untied his arm from the chain. Santoro whizzed up beside him and then, with an awful lot of creaks and groans, Boja followed. He had a length of chain around each wrist and ankle. Rails stood on his belly, pulling the central length as if he was riding a big furry elevator up to the top floor.

'FLYING!' Boja beamed in delight.

'The bear could do with eating a few less breakfasts!' Rails wheezed.

Once Rails had jumped off, Dev and Santoro grabbed Boja's paws and pulled him to safety. 'Where's Brianne?' Dev shouted, staring back down into the smoky mess of lights below.

'I think I'm getting the hang of this armour!' Brianne

suddenly cried, roaring out from the smoke. Her flember armour was blazing, the triple-powered boss rocket on her back blasting bright, dancing flames out behind her. She clamped onto the wall like a sticklebug, barely able to hide her excitement.

'Everything I do feels ten times stronger, ten times faster!' she laughed, scrambling up the wall and then out through the hole in the Foundry roof. 'I feel like I could take on the whole CITY!'

She stopped, staring across the outskirts with a look of shock on her face. Dev was first to climb up behind her. He leant over the edge of the Foundry, looking down to the streets below where he saw a mob of Lessers wading through the flashing red lights. They were holding sticks, poles, anything they could get their hands on. Anything they could use to attack the droids.

They were shouting.

They were *furious*.

Two of the Lessers, Pipo and Dollop from the races, caught sight of Brianne looking down at them. They started calling out her name. Within seconds everyone was chanting.

'BRIANNE! BRIANNE! BRIANNE!'

'They've had enough.' Rails beamed, proudly putting an arm around Brianne's shoulders. 'Everyone's had

enough of Prosperity! And it's all because of you!'

'If only they had flember armour too,' Dev whispered to himself. Another idea started to bubble away inside his mind. He caught his brother's eye. Santoro opened his mouth to object, but then only lightly shook his head in resignation.

Dev looked back down to the streets with a thrill in his veins.

'You'd all be *unstoppable*.' He grinned.

26
Raising an Army

With piles of powerless droids now filling the streets, Dev had a whole load of flember circuits to work with. Soon, however, it became clear this would be much too big a job for him to complete on his own, so the other, smaller foundries around the outskirts opened their doors too. Their fires blazed. Their chimneys smoked. Their blacksmiths hammered furiously into the night.

'She knows what we're up to,' Rails said, while he measured up a Lesser, and Dev clamped a flemberthyst into their chest. 'Grace, I mean. You said so yourself – she always seems to know what's going to happen.'

'I wondered about that, but why then would she send

all these police droids out here just for us to take them apart?' Dev muttered, a clucklewidget clamped between his teeth.

'It just feels wrong.' Rails shook his head. 'It feels like we're walking into a trap.'

'We won't be walking.' Brianne stood in the Foundry doorway, brightly lit by her own flember armour. 'We're going to tear through however many droids she sends at us, and then I'm going to *steal* that stupid old skull.'

Rails cast her a worried glance.

'We should have stormed the city a long time ago.' Brianne sniffed, stepping aside to let the newly armoured Lesser out of the Foundry. 'We should have done this instead of playing their silly games.'

It was midnight before Dev had a chance to step outside for some fresh air. Building flember armour for nearly everyone on the outskirts had taken a long time and now he was *exhausted*. But he still had his own armour to fix up, and he was deep in concentration twiddling a fiddlespork into his side panels when he heard his brother calling out to him.

'Fi-i-i-inally.' Santoro sat upon one of the rooftops opposite, resting his head against Boja's huge, heaving belly while the bear snored noisily behind him. 'You

know, you work too hard, Dev.'

Dev's eyes lit up at the sight of them both. 'Santoro! Where have you been?' He smiled wearily. 'I haven't seen you for ages!'

'Oh, we've been busy.' Santoro yawned, stretching out his arms. 'Boja's been carrying piles of armour from one forge to another . . .'

Boja snort-farted at the sound of his own name.

'And I've been going with him, overseeing the black-smiths, making sure everyone's working to your plans.'

Dev chuckled. 'I think you're enjoying this.'

'Maybe a bit.' Santoro smiled. 'I was the Youth Guild leader back in Eden, remember. Telling people what to do was part of the job!'

Dev climbed a barrel, then got up onto the roof and perched alongside his brother. 'Thank you for letting us stay for a bit longer. If I can just help Brianne get the skull, then there'll be more than enough flember for *everyone*.'

He smiled at the thought of it.

Then his smile wavered.

'I didn't mean to drag you after me, Santoro.' He sighed. 'I'm sorry you got drawn into all this.'

'Oh, this wasn't up to you, Dev! I *chose* to come.'

'And we're glad you did. Both of you.' Brianne stood

in the street below, arms folded, her flember armour flickering. 'You've only been here a day, but you've already helped us so, so much. Thanks to you, Dev, we can copy their flember armour. Now we have an equal playing field at least. Now we have a *chance*.'

Other Lessers ambled around her in their half-finished armour.

'You're the one who won two of their races,' Dev laughed. 'You were the inspiration everyone needed.'

The Lessers mumbled in agreement.

Brianne looked a little awkward. 'I mean . . . I just don't think it's fair that the Primes should keep all of Prosperity's flember for themselves. It's not fair they should grow the best food, and live in the most comfortable surroundings, while we live out here in the dust.'

More Lessers gathered.

'They make us race against them just for the chance to be equal.' A confidence swelled in Brianne's voice. 'They beat us time after time and say it's proof that our flember is weaker than theirs. And even when *I won*, they threw me out of Prosperity for it!'

The other Lessers grew angry at the thought of it. Weapons were lifted into the air, torches, spare arms, anything they had to hand.

Brianne prowled back and forth like a wildcat.

'And all because they say their flember is better than ours?' she yelled. 'Well, not any more! We'll march into their city. We'll TAKE their skull! And then everyone in Prosperity will be treated EQUALLY!'

The Lessers burst into applause. Dev joined in, his heart swelling at the sight of Brianne striding around so proudly, so fiercely. His brother too became thoroughly caught up in the moment, clapping so hard it made Boja fart himself awake.

'You did good, Dev,' Santoro shouted over the crowd. 'Maybe that book of yours brought you here for a reason!'

Dev slipped the backpack from his shoulder, then carefully pulled the flember book out. 'Maybe it did,' he agreed, clutching it fondly between his hands.

But it felt different.

It felt slightly *lighter*.

The cover was still the same, its golden F still gently crackling with flember, but when he flipped it open he saw not the bundle of pages he was expecting, but a completely different book inside.

All the colour drained from his cheeks.

'Someone stole my book!' he gasped.

27
The Heist

'Uhhh . . . we may have a problem!' Rails called from further down the street. He beckoned the Lessers to follow him and they did, proudly clanging and clomping between the houses in their new flember armour. Santoro too was quick to jump from the roof and follow, while Boja sleepily rolled himself upright, snorted something about breakfast, and sleepily trudged his way along behind.

'Are you coming, Dev?' Santoro called back.

Dev looked up, discarded the recipes for Hufflepig Pie, then slipped the covers of the flember book inside his backpack. 'I know I had the flember book until we were inside the library,' he muttered, clambering down from the roof. 'And the pages were still in there, I'm sure of it. Then *Plops* took the book, but it wouldn't have had time to make the switch as Santoro was too close behind. In fact, the only other time I lost sight of the book was when Boja fell through the floor and I couldn't find it. Not until—'

He froze at the realization.

'Grace!' he cried. 'She must have found the flember book, switched the insides with the Hufflepig Pie book, and then wedged *that* into Plops' flember circuit. She made it look like an accident!'

He stumbled along at the tail end of the Lessers. 'That's what she's been up to! All this time she's been planning to steal the flember book. But why? Why would it be so important to her?'

Dev was so lost in his own thoughts that when Santoro stopped, Dev bumped straight into him.

'Dev, look,' Santoro whispered.

Dev raised his head towards the huge boundary of cables.

It seemed . . . *taller*.

'Has it . . . has it grown?' He gulped.

'I told you, she knows we're coming!' Rails sighed, forlornly stroking his beard.

Brianne seethed. 'She's used that skull of hers to wrap

more cables into the boundary!'

'And that's not all,' Rails added. He picked up a stone from the ground and flung it into the air above them. Instantly a cable spun out from the boundary, whipping the stone away with a loud WH-P-S-C-CHHHH!

Everyone gasped as one, especially Boja, who shuddered at the thought of where Prosperity's cables had once been poking him.

'There's no way we're climbing over,' Rails said, folding his arms across his flember armour. 'It would have been hard enough before, but now . . . now we don't have a chance.'

'They won't stop me,' Brianne growled, as her armour started to light up. 'Thanks to Dev's hard work, I bet I can just leap right over it.'

'You wouldn't make it.' Dev cleared his throat. 'I mean . . . even if you were firing your flember at max, which could be extremely dangerous, any one of those cables could take you out. No, we need another way to get everyone inside.'

'Or we might only need to get *one* person inside.' Rails grabbed a length of drainpipe, drew a sweeping line in the dirt with it and then the outline of the Spire above. 'This is the Spire, right?' He added a network of lines rising from beneath the building. 'The Spire pulls all its flember up from below ground, then sends it out all over Prosperity.'

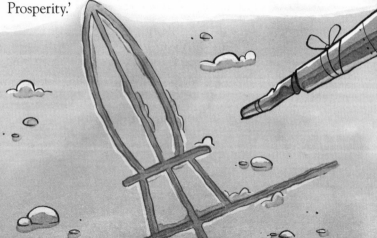

Brianne knelt down beside the drawing. 'Yeah, we know. And right now most of it is flowing through the boundary.'

'True,' Rails continued. 'But when the flember first comes into the Spire it goes straight up to the very top of it, like it's collecting somewhere.' He used his drainpipe to follow the line of flember all the way up through the Spire before drawing a circle at the very top.

'The Storm – Grace mentioned that before,' Dev gasped. 'It must house some kind of battery, to store Prosperity's flember until she decides where it should go.'

'That's what I'm thinking.' Rails nodded.

'A battery made of *gold*,' Dev exclaimed, kneeling down beside the lines in the dirt. 'Gold is the only material that can hold on to flember for a long enough time!' He thought back to the cables he'd seen at the very top of the Spire, the ones he had watched crackle and roll like a thundercloud when they first walked through the atrium. 'The battery *must* be inside the Storm,' he muttered under his breath.

'Hang on, Rails, how do *you* know all this?' Santoro objected. 'I thought Lessers stayed beyond the boundary.'

Rails slowly climbed back onto his feet. 'We helped build the Spire.' He sighed. Other Lessers shuffled behind him, the older weary Lessers, all awkwardly squeezed into their ill-fitting armour. 'The Primes were never going to get their hands dirty, were they? They needed us to do all the hard work and then, well, they gave us houses around the edge as a reward. Which was fine until the boundary appeared. Until our ground started drying up.'

'The Primes kept all the flember for themselves!' Dev exclaimed.

'But if someone could just get inside the Storm,' Rails added. 'Disrupt the flow of flember somehow . . .'

'. . . then the boundary will fall!' Brianne cried, leaping to her feet. 'And our whole army of Lessers can charge into Prosperity!'

The Lessers cheered at the very thought of it.

'But you've just said there's no way to get inside.' Santoro pointed his sword towards the bulging cables.

'How is even one person going to sneak into Prosperity?'

'I'll do it.' Dev stood, a nervous smile upon his lips. 'I've done it before.'

28
The Sewers, Again

H U-U-U-U-U-UUFFFFF!
Boja blew into the Sewer Ball, inflating it like bubblegum.

'That's enough.' Dev pinched the nozzle. 'It only needs to fit me.'

Boja hiccupped with surprise. 'I CAN COME!' he whimpered.

With a loud succession of SQUEAKs and FRRPs, Dev slipped the Sewer Ball over his head, dragging it down until it had reached his feet, at which point he rolled over into it. 'You can't go back inside Prosperity!' he called out from inside. 'The failsafe, remember? If Grace so much as sees you, Boja, the cables will start sucking out your flember again! It's too dangerous!'

Boja helplessly tried to mouth a protest, but let out a disgruntled fart instead.

'Dev, this is crazy.' Santoro pressed his hands against the ball. 'If you have to go back into Prosperity then *I'll* come with you. We'll work better as a team.'

'You need to stay out here and watch Boja,' Dev replied, tying the nozzle into a knot.

Santoro looked over to Boja, who was recoiling in disgust at the smell of his own bottom gas. 'But he's *fine*,' Santoro insisted, pinching his nose too. 'Everyone here will look after him while we're gone.'

'Boja's our *family*,' Dev whispered, rolling the Sewer Ball a little closer to his brother. 'If I get trapped inside Prosperity, then you might need to take him home.'

Anger choked Santoro's voice. 'Then I'll go through the sewers *instead* of you! I'm better at fighting than you are! I'll have a better chance getting through the Spire!'

Dev tried to hold his nerve. 'But I'm the one who knows how flember works,' he replied. 'So once I'm inside the Storm I should be able to figure out a way to shut it all down.'

Santoro growled in frustration while Dev leant forwards, rolling the Sewer Ball along the ground.

'Good luck.' Brianne nodded, as the Lessers looked on

behind her. 'The second, the very *second* that boundary falls we're all rushing inside.'

Boja reluctantly slid the unlocked manhole cover to one side as Dev wobbled closer, took a deep breath, then sank through the hole and dropped into the darkness with a loud, wet SQUELCH.

'Grace controls the Spire with her skull,' Rails shouted down. 'But the Storm is its heart. Go straight for the – hurgh – heart, and everything else will fall!'

Dev nodded.

Turned his ball round.

And then he started rolling through the filth.

29
Reinforcements

It wasn't easy controlling the Sewer Ball without Boja. The sticky, squelchy sludge slowed Dev down – it clung, it dragged him under if he didn't keep moving. He had hoped his own flember armour might help power him along but, despite his repairs, it too was struggling. It blinked and sparkled, sending rushes of flember through his arms and legs but only for brief moments. And only enough flember to lurch him a few rolls forward at a time.

Soon, however, by the flickering light of his own flemberthysts, he saw the iron rungs of a ladder embedded into the wall. He tilted the Sewer Ball's nozzle up, then carefully undid it, slowly squeezing himself out and dragging the floppy ball behind him as he climbed.

Up, through the manhole, and then out into the cool of night.

He gasped a few lungfuls of clean air, quickly washed and stuffed the ball inside his backpack, then started to sprint across the gardens. The daytime flowers had curled up to sleep, and a whole new array of colours had bloomed in their place. Pillipos, corneo lilies and dally-hoops grew across the vines, all of them blossoming into bizarre shapes the like of which Dev had only seen in the shadows of the Wildening. Insects buzzed, glowed and plipped across the ponds, between the fountains, a display of magical lights floating right before his eyes.

The fallen statue of the Second Pioneer, however, still lay crumbled across the lawns. Dev hopped between the rubble, then on towards the ebbing light of the Flember Stream. 'Just a straight ride up,' he panted, as the glass doors of the elevator SCHOOF-ed closed around him. 'All the way to the very top. Fifty-first floor.'

The elevator lifted away silently, carrying him up through the glowing, churning engine, up, through the central atrium, then suddenly screeched to a halt at the ground floor. The doors opened. Plops hovered outside, with row upon row upon row, of droids hovering behind it.

'Rule 003 – Prime citizens must not attempt to – BIBBLECRACKERS – overthrow civilization,' Plops insisted, the face upon its screen looking somehow more furious than ever.

Dev reluctantly stepped out, only for the elevator to suddenly abandon him, closing its doors and sinking

back down through the Flember Stream.

'Punishment will be – CUSTARD – SEVERE,' Plops warned as Dev faced the droids. These ones, however, weren't police droids. They were all the other droids from around the Spire. The waiter droids, still wearing their bow ties, the chef droids, the fire droids, the medic droids, even the two beeping droids from reception, who, to be fair, didn't look particularly comfortable with what was happening.

'I . . . I don't want any trouble,' Dev started. 'I just left something in the Spire. My *book*. I . . . I've come to get it back.'

'The First Pioneer is aware of your – FAT SOCKS – plans,' Plops warned, just as a loud chatter of noise drowned out its voice. It was coming from the balconies above. Dev turned to see a crowd of Prime citizens, each of them struggling to pull on their own flember armour, descending the steps towards the ground level, then running past Dev, past the droids, and out onto the concourse.

'They're not fighters,' Esco snarled, marching amongst them. 'But they might just be enough to get in the way. To slow your Lessers down from stealing all our flember.'

'It's not YOUR flember,' Dev snapped back. 'It never was! Flember's for *everyone*!'

'Mother told us about your plan,' Ralto growled from the other side, loudly clanging his claws together while Sienna rode on his shoulders. 'She told us that you'd come back into the Spire, that you'd try to drop the boundary.'

'There's no way she could have known that!' Dev whispered under his breath. He felt a cold sweat ripple across his skin. He couldn't fight three Primes, nor all the droids. He'd need to come up with a way out of this, another invention, something *ingenious* . . .

Just then a rather pungent smell filled his nostrils.

It smelled like rotting eggs, like muddy cheese, like a hufflepig enclosure that hadn't been cleaned out for two weeks. He clamped a hand to his mouth so he didn't throw up, then he swung around to see where it was coming from.

And there, in the elevator behind him, stood Boja.

His fur absolutely caked in filth.

Santoro perched carefully upon his head.

'He wad quide insisdent we come abder you,' Santoro said, a clothes peg pinching his nose. He drew his sword from its sheath with a quivering SCHI-I-I-INGGG! 'Eben if id meand walking through de sewers.'

'COOEEE!' Boja waved, so excited to see Dev that the smell barely seemed to register. 'Came to – hurgh – HELP!'

'HURGHHHH!' Esco shrieked, flushing green at the smell as he clutched his bulging cheeks. 'You . . . you savages. You're treading it EVERYWHERE!'

'You *did* call us sewer rats.' Dev grinned, turning to face them with a new-found confidence. 'So how else do you expect us to get inside?'

He fired up his flember armour, poised to run towards the droids, only for a huge, stinky, filth-covered Boja to bump him out of the way.

'Dev, ged to the Sdorm!' Santoro yelled, steering the bear by yanking on his ears.

'BWOOOOARGHH!' Boja agreed. Flember swirled across his arms, circled around his fists and blazed into huge beautiful gauntlets. He ploughed through the droids as if they were skittles. With the whiff of sewer filth still filling the air, neither Esco, Sienna nor Ralto could stomach getting too close. They could barely look at Boja without gagging, which suited Boja just fine.

'We can hold dem off as long as you need!' Santoro laughed.

'But the CABLES!' Dev cried. He'd already spotted one. It had kept to the very edges of the atrium, slither-ing, slowly unwinding, *stalking*. Waiting for its moment to strike Boja.

'We'll deal with them! Dev, GO!' Santoro shouted.

Dev spun around and leapt into the empty, but still rather stinky, elevator. 'RULE 014!' Plops dragged itself over a carpet of crushed droids. 'The Storm is – FRILLY BISCUITS – off limits to all but the First Pioneer!'

'Well, if she's already up there,' Dev closed the doors, 'then maybe I can get my book back too.'

30
The Storm

The elevator lifted silently through the glowing lights of the Flember Stream. This high up were the residential levels. Their balconies were empty. Dark. Only the pulsating ebb of flember lit them up.

Dev gulped nervously.

He suddenly felt very alone.

The doors stopped just short of the Storm, opening up onto a wide, circular platform. A spiralling staircase completed the journey. Dev placed a trembling hand upon its railing, peering down to see Santoro and Boja fighting the droids below. From this height they both looked as tiny as piddlebugs, but now Dev could see more cables circling them. They thrashed towards Boja, only for Santoro to steer the bear away each time.

Dev turned back to the Storm, puffed out his cheeks and steeled himself.

'Just . . . just get your book back, and bring down the boundary,' he muttered, climbing the steps. Cables slithered out from the Storm, brushing against his helmet, sparks of flember pattering against his nose. 'However this battery works I can disrupt it. I . . . I'm Dev! Dev P. Everdew! If there's one thing I'm good at doing, it's figuring out how things *work*!'

He took the last few stairs.

And then he stepped up, into the Storm.

It was beautiful inside the Storm. Quiet. Peaceful. A sea of glowing cables gently brushed around Dev's boots, his legs, his arms, as if they were welcoming him in. Sparkling blue lights glimmered in the air. They danced across his prickling skin, then sunk deep, deep into his bones.

He sighed with a feeling of utter bliss.

The cables curved up and around to form a huge, cavernous bubble. Then Dev noticed the *gold*, a framework of golden beams holding it all in place. 'The battery isn't inside the Storm,' Dev gasped. 'It IS the Storm.'

What floated in front of him, however, really took his breath away. Lines. Bright, glowing lines of flember. They drifted hazily in and out of each other to form a complex map of circles, ebbing and pulsing as it hung in the air.

Dev didn't know what it was, but it was *beautiful*.

'For all the brilliant workings of your young mind' – Grace stood beneath the lines, her shadow cast long by their glow – 'you're still blindly scrambling around in the mud. You don't understand our technology, our way of life. You've just blundered into the middle of it all.'

'I . . . I know you've got my book!' Dev bit his lip to hold his nerve. 'And . . . and there's a whole army of Lessers waiting outside the boundary, ready to charge into Prosperity, so you'd better give it back before—'

Grace turned, lifting the skull in both hands and holding it tantalizingly close towards Dev. 'You'll need this.' She smiled. 'Go on. Take it. Use it to control all of Prosperity's flember. You could drop the boundary. You could take what you need and go home.'

Dev reached out towards the skull, only to wonder why Grace was so ready to hand it to him. 'This is another of your tricks,' he muttered, pulling away. 'You know everything I'm going to do. You stole my book. You tricked us into the Wildening. Somehow you even knew we were building an army. You just don't seem surprised about *any* of it.'

Grace smiled her calm, unflustered smile and pulled the skull back towards her. 'Everything has to happen in the right order,' she said. 'You have done everything I was told you would do, exactly when you were supposed to do it.'

She stepped to one side. Behind her, Dev saw the opening of the Flember Stream pipe, a wide, bright hole from which all the cables fed. And there, above it, hung a small, round nest of threads.

And inside the nest sat a woman.

She looked old, incredibly old, even older than Dev's grandmother Ventillo (and she was *very* old). And yet she *glowed*. Her long hair sparkled with the glimmering light of flember. It floated gently around her face as if she were underwater, swaying against her wrinkled skin, across her thin lips, around the decorated antlers she wore upon her head.

She raised two large, black eyes towards Dev.

'You took your time,' she croaked. Then she clenched her bony fists and pulled the threads even tighter, wringing them of their flember as it trickled down her wrists. She took a deep, satisfied breath.

'I pulled this Lesser out of the Wildening years ago,' Grace proudly announced. 'Before Prosperity was even built. Those she left behind called her the Oracle. She has . . . powers, Dev. Abilities. She can *read* the Flember Stream. She reads it like a book. She can tell me *anything* that's happening *anywhere* on the island.'

She beamed with pride at Dev's stunned face. 'So I put her to work,' she said. 'Up here, at the top of the Spire. She's been plotting out a map of the Flember Stream just for me.'

Dev peered closer at the lines as they drifted past. He

saw finer details ripple across them, patterns, sparkling symbols like he'd seen in his book but far, far more detailed. More intricate. All of it pulsating as if it was pounding to a heartbeat.

'Every blossoming flower, every fluttering moth, every honking wilderpig,' Grace laughed. 'The Oracle can see it all from here!'

Dev stared again at the frail old lady floating in front of him, barely able to believe what he was hearing. 'Why . . . why would she help you?'

'She knows what I'll do to her friends in the Wildening if she doesn't.' A snarl crept into Grace's voice. 'You see, that floating old lady doesn't just see what's going on right now – she can also skip a few chapters. The Flember Stream shows her what's *going* to happen.'

'No one can know the future,' Dev croaked, before remembering all of the times Grace seemed to know what he was about to do before he did.

'The Oracle does!' Grace cried in delight. 'And she's told me I'm going to build NEW Prosperities! A whole line of cities, all along the Flember Stream! All of them controlled by the amazing, magical power of flember! Imagine it, Dev – I could finish what Cervantes Escobar never managed to do. I could finally bring civilization to the whole of Flember Island!'

She reached into her robes, and pulled out the bundle of pages she'd stolen from the flember book.

'My BOOK!' Dev gasped.

'It's not yours any more.' Grace cast a scowl towards the Oracle. 'You see, once we Pioneers had built Prosperity, I came to the Oracle to ask where next to place our cities,

where else the Flember Stream
reaches close enough to the surface that
we might tap into it. She refused to tell me. She said I
had to wait, that it was important to allow events to run
in the correct order if I wanted my plans to come to be.'

She held the pages out in front of her and grinned
excitedly. 'She said I had to wait for *you*. That *you* would
bring this book to Prosperity. And that I had to wait
until you were stood right here, at this very moment,
entirely of your own free will, and then I should do . . .
this.'

Suddenly she flung the pages up above her head.
They caught upon the lines of the flember map, dragged
around the circles as if being pulled into place.

Then the hidden lines upon each page started to
glow too.

One map revealed upon another.

Both now complete.

'THERE!' Grace exclaimed, pointing to the triangular symbols shining out from the pages of the flember book. 'There's another place I could reach the Flember Stream. And THERE! Another! Oh, Dev, look. LOOK! Now I know exactly where to build!'

Dev could barely believe what he was seeing, could barely comprehend that the pages of the flember book could be used in such a way. 'You've known all this from the start,' he gasped. 'You've been waiting to do this from the moment we got here!'

'Oh, well before then!' Grace laughed. 'The Oracle told me when you first filled that robot bear of yours with flember. All the way up there on that mountain, she saw it, she felt it rumble right through her. Just as she saw you break that big old Eden Tree. Then you and the bear rolling down through the Wildening, she saw that too. She told me of your bear's bottom blowing most of Darkwater apart. She saw you coming to Prosperity, to me, through the tunnels. She saw it *all*.'

She took a deep, satisfied breath.

'All I had to do was be *patient*.'

Grace seemed so delighted with herself, so happy that things were going exactly how she had been foretold that she didn't notice the large swell of cables rising behind her. But Dev did. He watched them split, breaking like a wave. He watched a huge red paw slip between them. Then a big black nose. POP! A big, bulging eyeball, whirling round in its socket until it caught sight of Dev. Then another eyeball, both of them squeezed up by two grinning cheeks.

'FOUND YOU!' Boja boomed, as Dev shrieked with delight.

The smell of the sewers hit Grace's nose.

'Waid, whad . . . whad's he doing here,' she boilked, sticking two fingers up her nostrils as she swung round to the Oracle. 'Dis isn'd supposed to be happening! You told me de bear geds captured by de droids! You TOLD me.'

The Oracle cast a weary stare towards Grace.

She opened her thin lips to speak.

'I lied,' she said.

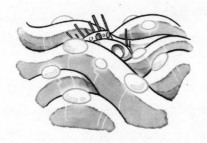

31
A New Guardian

Dev leapt through the Storm, from one golden strut to another. He grabbed Boja's paw and helped the bear to haul himself up. 'The cables,' he asked. 'Didn't they hurt you?'

'Cables . . . LIFTED me,' Boja said with a grin, crawling onto his paws as a number of cables pushed his bottom up and into the Storm.

Grace's pale cheeks flushed red.

'Dey . . . dey lifded you?' she scowled. 'Bud I didn't make dem do dat!' She yoinked her fingers from her nostrils and clutched the glowing skull firmly.

'It must be broken!' she cried, shaking it furiously. 'It's not WORKING!'

'The skull only worked as long as I let it.' The Oracle was glowing brighter now, her hair swirling like flames. 'I've watched, patiently, while you have misused the Flember Stream, while your actions have caused a great imbalance. For *too long* I have allowed you to steal flember from where it belongs.'

Cables lunged towards Grace. One knocked the skull spinning from her hands, more wrapped around her wrists. 'Get OFF me!' She writhed. 'This isn't supposed to HAPPEN!'

Dev cautiously let go of Boja's paw and edged across the sparkling cables, closer to the Oracle, his heart pounding in his chest as he stood below her. 'You're controlling Prosperity's flember?' he asked.

Despite her bright, beautiful glow, the Oracle looked like she was struggling. Her breaths were short. Tears glistened in her eyes. 'I am now,' she whispered. 'But this is too much flember for a frail old body like mine to hold for long, I had to wait for just the right moment . . .'

'Well, maybe . . . maybe I can redirect the flember!' Dev cried. 'That's what I came up here to do, after all. I've worked with flember before, I *invented* Boja—'

The Oracle's lips cracked into an affectionate smile. 'Oh, I know the strengths inside you, Dev,' she said. 'I have watched you every step of the way. I have felt every height you have fallen. Every tear you've shed. I've heard every beat of your heart across this long, painful journey. I have seen the things you do not yet know you are capable of.'

'Then let me help you,' Dev insisted.

'You already have,' she replied. 'You came here.'

Dev became aware of the cables around him. They were agitated, writhing and thrashing against each other, their flemberthysts glowing brightly with flember.

'What do you mean?' Dev asked, turning back to the Oracle. 'What's all this for? Why go to all this trouble just to bring me here?'

The Oracle leant forwards, stretching the glowing threads behind her.

'Because the *bear* follows you.'

Suddenly more cables spun out, wrapping around Boja, around his wrists, his ankles, his ample bottom. Flember raced across his fur, glowing behind his eyes, sparkling out from his nostrils. And then, to Dev's amazement, the cables started to lift the bear right off his feet.

'What . . . what are you doing to him?' Dev cried.

'Boja is the only one who can restore balance,' the Oracle's voice declared from inside the bright, almost blinding light of her nest. 'But his body had to be fixed first, to be strengthened, if he was ever to hold this much flember.' As she spoke, flember channelled along the cables and sank into Boja's fur. Faster it went, and brighter, and faster, and brighter. Boja's failsafe spun so fast it cracked, splitting the circuit-breaker from his chest and the straps from across his shoulders. Soon he was glowing so much he had become an x-ray of himself, the shadow of his heart DOOMPF-DOOMPF-DOOMPF-ing away inside his chest.

Dev stumbled backwards, shielding the light from his eyes. 'I don't understand,' he cried, his voice lost beneath the deafening rush of flember. '*Please!* Don't hurt him!'

Lights spun around, dazzling and disorientating, everything so bright and so loud until only one voice could be heard.

'Do not fear for your friend,' the Oracle whispered as if she were inside Dev's head. 'Only Boja can put this flember back where it belongs, but *you* will need the courage to help him.'

'I don't know how!' Dev yelled back.

'You'll figure it out,' the Oracle replied. 'I've already seen how it happens.'

And then, just as suddenly as it had started, it all stopped.

Silence fell.

Dev un-scrunched his eyes. The map was gone. The Oracle was gone. Her nest too was gone, only thin wisps of it left floating upon the air. In her place, however, he saw Boja, bright, shining Boja, bursting with flember as he hovered above the haze of the Flember Stream. Cables swam around him, each of them carrying great washes of flember in and out of his buttocks.

He looked down at Dev and smiled.

'All of Prosperity's flember.' Dev raised a hand towards the glowing bear. 'It's all flowing through your BUM.'

'Tickles,' Boja agreed, before hiccupping out a plume of sparkles.

32
An Abandoned Dream

Grace emerged from a mesh of cables, rubbing her eyes furiously. 'Where IS she?' she demanded. 'The ORACLE! That lying, scheming ORACLE! Where did she GO?'

Then her face fell.

'My MAP!' she cried, staggering around, snatching the loose pages of the flember book as they fluttered down around her. 'She took my MAP! These aren't enough. I can't read THESE!' She waggled the pages furiously as if the map might light back up across them.

'YOU!' she snapped at Dev. 'YOU can read these pages.'

'Not without flember.' Dev folded his arms defiantly.

'And the Oracle gave all the city's flember to Boja. She told him to put it back where it belongs!'

A look of pure thunder rolled across Grace's face as she squinted up at the brightly lit Boja. 'That's *impossible*.' She scowled. 'The Oracle wouldn't give control of Prosperity to that . . . that thing. That old pile of scrap metal. That tatty, filth-covered beast!'

'Harumph,' the glowing Boja sulked.

'His *name* is Boja,' Dev replied. 'And if you don't mind, I'll have my book back now.'

He stepped out to take the pages, only to suddenly lose his footing. The cables beneath him were splitting apart, disentangling themselves from the golden frame. The walls too started to crack open. Before Dev could even get off his knees, all the cables of the Storm had drooped open and the cold night air was rushing in around him.

Beneath a twinkling sky, the fifty-first floor of the Spire opened out like a blossoming flower.

Dev glanced down, across the whole of Prosperity, from the gardens to the outskirts, and the thick cables of the boundary in between.

The thick *sagging* cables.

'Boja,' he gasped. 'Boja, are *you* collapsing the boundary?'

From somewhere inside the bright, Boja-shaped

light above him, Dev heard a giggle. He crawled closer to the edge, watching Lessers spill in over the cables, BLAST-ing and WOOSH-ing and CLANK-CLANK-CLANK-ing their way into the gardens and up, towards the concourse. The armoured Primes ran to head them off, but then they all just . . . stopped. They turned their heads to see what the Lessers were pointing at. And they stared at the huge glowing bear high above the Spire.

'You've destroyed *everything*.' Grace suddenly yanked Dev backwards by his scarf. 'You and your . . . *monster*! You've ruined everything the Pioneers worked so hard to create. You've crumbled my new cities into dust before I could even build them!'

She held the crumpled pages of the flember book out in front of her, over the long, long drop to the ground.

Malice flashed across her eyes.

'Give the pages back!' Dev scrambled to his feet and leapt towards Grace. She lifted the pages even higher. 'I need my map,' he pleaded. 'I need it to get HOME!'

Grace stared down at him coldly. 'You're a clever lad,' she replied, flinging the pages out onto the wind. 'You'll find another way.'

33
The Climb Back Down

Dev lunged for the pages without thinking, the tip of his boots scraping along the very edge of the cables until suddenly there was nothing beneath him.

And he was falling.

Everything rushed past in a blur. Dev couldn't scream, could barely take a breath. His teeth clenched, his heart pounded, his armour crackled with flember as all of Prosperity rushed up towards him. Then, with a loud THUMP, he hit something hard. At first he barely dared open his eyes. But when he did, he saw a thick white cable quivering beneath him.

'Your monster! Your . . . your BEAR!' Grace shrieked from the top of the Spire. Dev looked up to see her wrapped in cables, staring wildly towards Boja. Bright, blazing Boja. Cables were not only plugged into his buttocks but also now clenched between his paws, writhing out around him like a dazzling display of arms, swooping down around the Spire and holding Dev high above the city.

It took Dev a moment to catch his breath, even to manage any words. 'B . . . Boja,' he stammered. 'You caught me!'

'CAUGHT . . . you!' Boja let out a loud, booming chuckle that rattled through every window of the Spire. Then, suddenly, his expression changed. His cheeks ballooned out. His eyes bulged in their sockets.

The cable beneath Dev slackened, dropping him down a couple more levels of the Spire.

'What's wrong, Boja?' Dev shouted, struggling to hold on.

'LEARNING . . . HOW TO . . .'

The cable flopped completely. Dev was flung into the sky and then – THUMP! – he hit another cable. This cable too was sagging, but the sheer momentum of his fall propelled him onto his feet and sent him running down the length of it.

And as he ran, his armour kicked in.

Flember surged through his body, supercharging his legs and leaping him out over the perilous drop. THUMP! With a loud GA-A-A-A-A-ASP of relief he landed on the nearest cable. His whole body was shaking. His lungs bursting. But thanks to the flickering flemberthysts clamped across his armour, Dev felt AMAZING.

He waved up towards Boja, just as a page from the

flember book flapped past his nose.

'The book!' Dev yelped, swiftly grabbing the page, then scouring the skies for others. In a blur of glowing blue lights he was gone, leaping towards the next cable, snatching another page before accidentally skidding off the end of it.

THUMP!

Another cable rose to catch him.

'Thank you, Boja!' he yelled.

The glowing bear at the top of the Spire grinned back. 'HNNNNGGGG!' he strained, using all his might to swoop the cable around, then slide Dev down a few more levels. Another page. A drop, then THUMP! Another cable. Dev stumbled. His armour was struggling – he could feel it. What he'd done to patch it up wasn't holding, and now some of its flemberthysts were fading.

'I can fix this!' He wrenched the blackrock wires from his breastplate and knotted them down inside his boots. A rush of flember washed down to the very tips of his toes. 'I can *improve* it!'

SLAM! A cable knocked Dev out into the air. He heard a distant 'SOHH-REEEE!' from Boja, only for another cable to catch him, inadvertently smearing his face down the outside glass of the Spire. Level thirty-five. Level thirty-four. Level thirty-three. Then it flopped again. Dev grabbed a cluster more pages caught against the windows then, with all of his flember redirected back into his legs, he leapt away from the Spire.

Out into the sky.

Another page. A cable. A page. Another flember-thyst failed. Dev rerouted more of his own flember. It made him feel dizzy, or rather, *dizzier*, as all the flember drained from his upper half. Another page. Leap, and a cable. Level twenty-two. Level twenty-one. Cable. Cable. Another page!

'THANK YOU, BOJA!' Dev laughed. He was almost enjoying it now. Another page. A long skid-d-d-d down along a drooping cable and then . . .

The cables ran out.

Dev slammed into the Spire somewhere between levels eleven and eight, smashing through the glass and rolling across the floor. 'YAHHHHHHH!' he yelled, helplessly somersaulting through what looked to be the Lysium Fields, as plumes of pink and orange petals billowed up behind him. And then, just as suddenly as it had appeared, the ground was gone again. Dev rolled between the railings and out, over the central atrium, bouncing off the Flember Stream pipe like a pinball and ricocheting down off the bridges. Level seven. Level five. Level two.

CRUNCH!

Ground level.

Dev's armour smashed into pieces, most of its flember-thysts shattering into dust. He took a moment, just a moment, for his flember to sink back beneath his skin, for his brain to stop spinning inside his head, before slowly, painfully, heaving himself up onto his knees.

'I got it,' he croaked, looking proudly down at the flember pages tightly clutched between his white knuckles. 'I got the flember book!'

Suddenly a pained ROAR-R-R-R echoed down through the Spire.

'Boja!' Dev cried, stuffing the pages into his backpack, then scrambling onto his feet. He ran across the glass floor, through a carpet of crumpled, battered droids, past the reception droids hiding behind their desk. Out, onto the concourse, in amongst the crowd of Primes and Lessers who were all staring, aghast, at the skies above them.

'DEV!' Santoro shouted, a sparking, fizzing Plops impaled on his sword. He threw the sword down and wrapped Dev into a tight hug. 'Dev, what HAPPENED up there?'

ROAR-R-R-R-R! it came again, even louder than before.

'Boja's in pain,' Dev yelled. 'He's in PAIN!'

There came another loud THUMP as one of the cables slumped onto the concourse. As it unfurled, Grace rolled out. She looked haggard, defeated, as pale and as shocked as someone who had just been swung down fifty-one floors by a bear-controlled cable.

'The BEAR!' she gasped, staggering to her feet. 'That BEAR stole Prosperity's flember!'

Dev stepped back to see the very top of the Spire, to see Boja, floating, burning as bright as the sun, an endless mesh of cables swaying out around him. The blinding light of flember crackled out across the skies as Prosperity itself was cast into an unnatural daylight.

And Dev's heart sank.

'He's overloading,' he shouted. 'This is too much flember, even for BOJA!'

34
The Brightest Bear of All

A crowd gathered behind Dev and Santoro, a crowd of Primes and Lessers alike. Ralto, Esco and Sienna stood amongst them, along with Nerise, Rails and Brianne, all of them forgetting their battles for a moment as they stared up at the extraordinarily bright bear floating above the Spire.

'BOJA, LET GO!' Dev shouted. 'YOU'RE TAKING TOO MUCH FLEMBER!' He could feel a lump rising in his throat. A panic running through his veins. He frantically gripped his brother. 'I have to get back up there,' he cried. 'I have to help Boja!'

'Dev, you barely survived coming down!' Santoro snapped. 'You can't go back up!'

'I have to do SOMETHING,' Dev sobbed. He spun round, clonking his fist against his helmet as if trying to knock his thoughts together. 'What did the Oracle say?' he muttered to himself. 'Balance! She said only Boja could restore balance. But did she mean balance for Prosperity, or—'

The answer hit him like a speeding hufflepig.

He ran through the crowd to the very far edge of the concourse, to where Boja might just be able to see him. 'BOJA!' he shouted, waving his arms frantically. 'BOJA, PUT THE FLEMBER BACK INTO THE *FLEMBER STREAM*!'

'What? NO!' Grace yelled, a little wobbly on her feet. 'That's OUR flember! It belongs to *Prosperity*!'

Two droopy cables rose from the gardens. They slid across the concourse, scattering the crowd as they flomped before Dev. One of the cables affectionately stroked his cheek, while the other dipped into a discarded bag of bufflechips. 'Put all the flember back where it belongs,' Dev pleaded to the cables. 'Just like you did with the Eden Tree, remember? Let it sink beneath the ground and find its own way, without anyone trying to control it. We can find the Flember Stream somewhere else. Then . . . then we can go home for *waffles*!'

'WAF-F-FLES,' Boja's voice echoed across Prosperity.

'Dev.' Santoro gripped Dev's arm. 'Does Boja seem to be getting . . . brighter?'

Dev held a hand above his eyes. Boja *was* growing brighter. And brighter. And BRIGHTER. Before long the Spire itself vanished from view, as did the cables, as did Prosperity itself, until all Dev could see around him was blinding white light.

'Boja, please,' he whispered. 'Please just put the flember *back*.'

Suddenly another almighty roar echoed through Prosperity. It rattled through Dev's bones, through the gardens, exploding every pane of glass out from the Spire. Boja's glimmering shadow dropped like a huge sack of whetherparsnips straight down inside the Flember Stream, down, through the central atrium of the Spire, pulling all the cables in with him, dragging them from the gardens, the fallen boundary, from the outside of the Spire itself. The Spire plunged into darkness one level at a time, the light from the Flember Stream disappearing down, down beneath the machine, right back down inside the earth.

Where it belonged.

Smoke billowed out through the Spire's main entrance as a huge pile of rubble, cables and glass crashed along with it. Prosperity's citizens huddled as one, coughing

and spluttering, but Dev couldn't wait. He grabbed the discarded bag of bufflechips and ran towards the Spire. 'BOJA!' he yelled, clambering over the rubble. 'BOJA, WHERE ARE YOU?'

What had once been the atrium was now a mess. The central pipe had collapsed, its surrounding bridges brought smashing to the ground. The rising line of balconies too had nearly been destroyed, shredded by the tangle of powerless cables pulled through them and down, into the ground, like an enormous torn cobweb.

Dev was struck by a heavy sense of dread. 'Boja?' he whimpered. 'Boja, are you in here?'

'We'll find him.' Santoro climbed in behind, heaving great chunks of rock away. 'Wherever he is, Dev, we'll find him.'

'We all will!' Brianne exclaimed, as she, Rails and a gaggle of Lessers all joined the search. Then Primes too. Not, perhaps, those who had lost the most from what had just happened – namely Grace and her children – who stayed at a distance upon the concourse. But the others. Prosperity's citizens rooted through he rubble in the dusty, flickering darkness, with only the gentle glow of their flember armour to light the way.

'We came here looking for flember,' Dev whispered. 'But right now I'd do anything just to have Boja back.'

He stopped. There, in the very middle of the rubble, he could see a light. It was gentle, it was ebbing, but it was there. 'BOJA!' Dev cried. Others rushed to help, pulling the wreckage away to reveal a rather crumpled, dusty-looking bear underneath. Dev heaved one big red eyelid open, then the other, only for them to both droop back down again.

'Please be OK,' Dev sobbed, burying his head in the bear's fur. 'Please please *please* be OK.'

Suddenly Boja's big black nose twitched.

His nostrils widened.

'Bufflechiiiips,' he murmured.

'Bufflechips!' Dev cried, hauling the bag from his pocket and pouring a stream of bufflechips into Boja's open mouth.

Boja noshed contentedly.

'Bufflechiiiips.'

'He's OK!' Dev yelled to the cheers of the crowd. 'Boja's OK!'

'I'd say he's better than OK.' Santoro knelt down. 'Just look at him, Dev!'

Dev gazed down at the ruffled bear. Flember crackled across Boja's fur, not just a little, but a lot, sparkling from his ears, his chewing lips, his fingertips. It crackled across his belly. It glimmered upon his bufflechip burps.

'I kepsch schome flember,' Boja mumbled through mouthfuls of chips. 'For the Edenschtree.'

'Oh, Boja!' Dev laughed. 'We can go home. We can finally go HOME!'

35
Grace's Greatest Lie

Esco stood upon the far reaches of the rubble, trying to straighten what was left of his tatty cape. 'You're leaving NOW?' he shouted with a manic tinge in his voice. 'You DESTROYED Prosperity, your monster sinks our flember down beneath the ground so NO ONE can have it, and NOW you're going home?'

'Not a monster,' Boja grumbled between licks of bufflechip dust.

'It was never Prosperity's flember in the first place.' Dev stood, his armour hanging off him in bits. 'All this time, Prosperity's been *stealing* it from the Flember Stream.'

'We USED it.' Ralto clanged his claws together. 'Primes brought flember up through the engine and made it work for us. That's our reward for finding it!'

'You stole flember away from the outskirts – the land there is barren and lifeless because of you!' Santoro shouted back. 'You made sure the Lessers couldn't have any. You STOLE it.'

Sienna climbed alongside her brothers. She stared at Dev silently from across the rubble, fists clenched, her

arm blades glinting by the light of her flemberthysts as if she was preparing to launch an attack.

Dev nervously bit his lip. He wasn't sure he had the strength left to defend himself.

Suddenly, from across the rubble, Brianne cried in delight. 'I GOT IT!' She beamed, holding up the battered, dented skull of Cervantes Escobar. 'I TOLD you I was going to come into Prosperity and—'

Her voice fell. She had noticed how not a single light flickered, nor glowed, from inside the skull.

'I think it's broken,' she muttered.

'There's no flember left for it to control,' Dev said. 'The skull has no power without flember.'

'And with the boundary down the skull can't keep us apart any more,' Rails added. 'Prime, Lesser, we may not have flember to share, but we *can* share Prosperity.'

'There's no such thing anyway,' Nerise, the chief science officer, spoke a little louder than perhaps she'd been intending. She looked up, shocked. 'Did I . . . did I say that out loud?'

'What do you mean, no such thing?' Brianne edged closer.

Nerise cleared her throat. 'Well, um . . . it's just that Prime flember, and Lesser flember. They're just words. That's all. They don't actually *exist*.'

There was a stunned silence. Everyone turned to stare at Grace. Grace didn't look back. She was sitting upon the rubble, a broken version of her former self. Her hair hung loose and messy, her gown was torn and her limbs looked so terribly thin. She was shivering, whether from the shock, or the cold of the night, or most likely both.

'Lies,' she muttered under her breath. 'It's all lies. How could anyone design and build a city as magnificent as Prosperity if there wasn't *Prime flember* flowing through their heart?' Her mutters rose into shouts. 'There was nothing here but old ruins when we started, now we have *civilization* . . .' Her voice waned as she gazed up at the dark, dusty remains around her.

'You *tested* us.' Rails lifted his harness towards Nerise, to show the bright glow of flember on his wrist. 'Your droids told us we were Lesser.'

'We ran blood tests on you,' Nerise sighed, clutching her head in her hands. 'I'm so sorry, but that's all we did. From the results we could tell who you were related to. If you matched to a bloodline we had on our register, then—'

'All Primes are the descendants of Cervantes Escobar!' Grace boomed, snatching the skull from Brianne's hands. 'He brought Prime flember to this island. We have a DUTY to put it to good use!'

A murmur of discontent rumbled through the citizens of Prosperity. Those who had been called Lessers looked shocked, as did the Primes, all of them united in their feelings of having been absolutely duped.

'I KNEW it!' Dev yelled excitedly. 'I thought it sounded odd. Primes and Lessers, indeed. Flember's universal! It's shared, between all of us!'

'This is outrageous!' Esco's long, pointy face scrunched down into a furious scowl. 'Anyone can tell we're superior to the Lessers! Our flember is remarkable. Our flember is PRIME!'

'Then how come I won two of your stupid races?' Brianne grinned, delighting in the moment.

Grace opened her mouth to protest, but Brianne wasn't finished.

'You made us race so we'd feel like things were fair. But they never were. Prosperity only ever favoured those who already had so much.' She opened her arms towards the rather nervous-looking Prime crowd. 'All we ever wanted was a city where everyone was treated equally. And now . . . we will *have* it.'

She lifted her harness high, so everyone could see the bright, glowing flemberthyst inside it.

'Flember won't divide us any more. Flember will be what *unites* us.'

One by one, the bewildered crowd around her lifted their harnesses above their heads too. A sea of floating, glowing lights, all united by flember.

Santoro raised his.

Boja raised his.

'That's IT!' Dev suddenly cried, raising his harness too. 'I know how to do it! I know how we can *rebuild* Prosperity!'

INVENTION 509: The Flember Ring

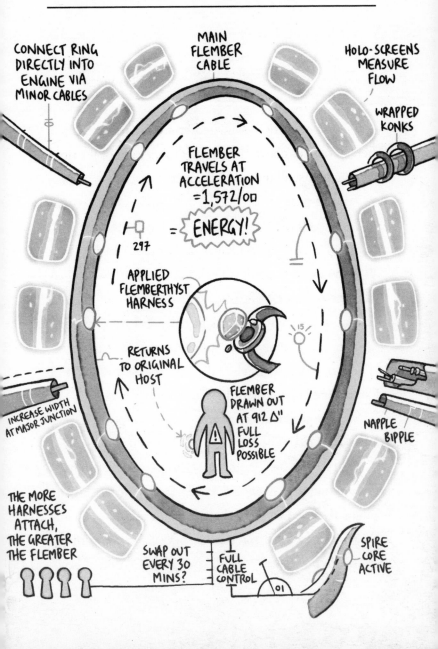

36
A New Way Forward

Dev adjusted the last few screens along the wall. A large crowd had gathered around him, all of them curious how exactly this big idea of his was going to work. 'Prosperity was built by three Pioneers,' Dev announced. 'The First Pioneer designed the city, the Second Pioneer found flember, and then the *Third* mechanized it all.'

Santoro stood, arms folded, at the front of the crowd. 'Dev, what exactly—'

'Everything they built together, everything you need to run the city, is already here,' Dev continued. 'The cables are lined with flemberthysts. You have an engine below your feet. All you need to get everything running again is a power source – all you need is an awful lot of *flember*!'

He smiled proudly. 'And Prosperity already has *loads* of it.'

He lifted his arm and pressed his harness against the main cable, watching as his flember billowed out and across its flemberthysts. A gentle glow flickered onto the screen above. The glow then trailed across, onto the next screen. And across to the next. And the next and the next, a very faint, thin line being dragged from flemberthyst to flemberthyst, circling all the way around the atrium, behind the crowds and back again. 'This is my flember.' Dev's voice faltered. His head started to swim. 'The flemberthysts are pulling it out of my body and it's making me feel weak. But if we *all* share our flember, then—'

Brianne stepped forward. She pressed her harness next to Dev's, watching with a smile as her flember started to flow out from it. The thin glowing line running along the Flember Ring thickened, just a little. Santoro was next, then Rails, Pipo and Dollop, then Nerise. More and more of the crowd surged forwards to help. Soon the Flember Ring was thick, bulging, bright with the light of their combined flember.

And Dev started to feel stronger again.

'Boja?' he called out.

'Helping.' He beamed, holding his harness against the Flember Ring. The flember line suddenly plumpened, and as it did, the engine beneath their feet started to turn. Glowing blue flember washed between the pulleys and pumps, pinging the proppleblops as they ground back into action. Lights flickered up through the atrium. Fountains started sprinkling across the gardens. The half-finished experiments of the Development Rooms whooshed and exploded. Whatever had been left cooking in the kitchens finally set off a smoke alarm.

Beneath the dark skies of early morning, the whole Spire lit up once again.

'It works,' Dev beamed. 'The city's being powered by *all* of our flember!'

'Dev, it's amazing,' Brianne said. 'But . . . well, we can't all stand here *for ever*!'

'You don't need to.' Dev pulled his harness away and stepped back. The crowd watched in amazement as a faint waft of sparkling flember drifted out after him. 'Just take it in turns, only a few of you at a time will be needed to keep the momentum going.' He sighed happily as his own flember sank beneath his skin. 'When you walk away your flember will always come back to you. You're just sharing it with everyone else for a little bit.'

Rails slapped his head in delight. 'I told you! That boy

is a GENIUS. Maybe he's the FOURTH PIONEER!'

'Maybe he is!' Brianne agreed. 'Dev, what you've given
to Prosperity is going to change this city for ever!'

Dev felt his cheeks flush red. Boja noticed it too.

'Bobbleberry!' He giggled. 'Dev's a bobbleberry!'

'I'm . . . I'm not a bobbleberry, and I'm not a Pioneer
either,' Dev replied bashfully. 'I . . . I'm just . . .'

'He's my *brother*.' Santoro proudly wrapped an arm
across Dev's shoulders. 'And he's incredible.'

37
A Few Moments Before Bed

'I still can't believe how much she *lied*.' Santoro walked out onto the concourse. The early morning was still dark, but it smelled sweet, like a million happy memories drifting on the breeze. 'Grace, I mean. She lied to every-one here about their flember, and she kept up the lie for *years*. Just so she could be in charge of them all.'

Dev sat, legs dangling over the gardens, watching all the glowing insects as they hovered between the trees. Now everyone was working together to rebuild the Spire he had managed to find a little time to himself. And, of all the citizens of Prosperity who had chosen to take over the jobs previously held by droids, it was those working in the kitchens who had taken to it with the most relish.

To celebrate this new era for the city they had whipped up all manner of treats and delights, which Dev now had a plateful of, and was gratefully enjoying.

'She lied to us too.' Dev munched into his last flopnut-topped bibbitz cracker. 'She never wanted to help us. She only wanted to keep me here long enough so she could steal the flember book. Maybe the Oracle was right. Maybe it was supposed to all happen like this.'

'Well, it's done now.' Santoro sat down and shuffled alongside his brother. 'And Boja's come out of it with all the extra flember you want, so we can go home. The three of us together, we'll be able to take anything the Wildening throws at us.'

Dev turned back towards the Spire, to where a bright, sparkling Boja was propped up against the ground-floor doorway. He too had been enjoying the snacks, but as

usual he had enjoyed far too many of them at once.

Now the rather bloated bear looked somewhat queasy.

'G-U-R-R-R-RP!' Boja belched, surprising himself as much as anyone.

Santoro laughed, plucking a handful of lobbolcakes from Dev's plate. 'Just wait till Mum hears about all you've done out here, Dev. How you managed to power a whole CITY with flember. She'll be so proud of you. So, so proud of you.'

'I hope so.' Dev smiled. 'I can't *wait* to see her again.'

'Your bear has been farting out his own name!' Brianne walked up behind them both. She handed Dev a glass of bilbobo juice, and to Santoro, a greenberry cocktail. 'I'm not sure how, exactly, he's doing it, but it definitely sounds like his butt's saying BOH-JA.'

'Ate too m-m-much,' Boja groaned. 'Need sleepzzz.' Then he rolled onto his back. Legs in the air. Eyes closed. Nose whistling. A gentle snore from his lips.

His name farting out onto the breeze.

'We're leaving soon,' Dev said to Brianne. 'Me, Boja and Santoro. We're going home.'

Brianne looked a little sad. 'Yeah, I figured you would.' She sighed.

'There are lots of people waiting for us back in Eden,' Santoro said. 'We've already been away far too long.'

'Of course.' Brianne sniffed, raising a toast with her own glass of frothy mint dulap. 'Well then, while you're here I should take this chance to say thank you. We've been *very* lucky to have you all here, and you'd all be welcome to visit again any time you like.'

'I'd *love* to come back.' Dev raised his glass to hers.

'To another visit.' Santoro cheered. 'It would be interesting to see what you do to the place.'

The three of them sat for a while, chatting, laughing, and watching the moon slowly sink behind the city. Then, when there was nothing else to say, they all lay back and listened to the hum of Prosperity's flember rushing through the cables.

And it felt nice, just for a little while, for Dev not to think about anything at all.

Prosperity's Final Secret

There came a time when the faintest light of dawn started to glow beyond the horizon, and everyone agreed that if they were going to sleep, it would be wise to do it now. Dev, Brianne and Santoro all led a very sleepy Boja back inside the Spire, coaxing him with whatever stray bufflechips they could pluck out of his fur. They walked between the rubble, over the glowing, turning gears of the engine, climbed the makeshift ladders to the higher floors, and flopped onto the beds that had been laid out for everyone until proper quarters could be designated.

Santoro took to his bed.

Brianne took to hers.

Boja lay across three and swiftly fell asleep while mumbling about breakfast.

Dev sat for a while beside him, but he didn't feel tired.

Eventually he got up and crept back down the ladders to the ground level, out onto the concourse, then down the piles upon piles of discarded cables that now lay as a rather uneven set of steps into the gardens. The trees still rustling in the wind, the grass still wet underfoot, of all of Prosperity's glories, it was nature that had survived throughout.

Dev stepped upon the grass, pulled his scarf up against the chilly night breeze, and he took a walk.

'RULE 053, Primes must not – CABBAGE – patrol the gardens at night – FINGERCHIPS!'

'Plops!' Dev jumped, before peering into the shadows of what was once the boundary. 'I thought Santoro ran his sword through you!'

Plops' blinking, angry little face shone out from the darkness. But Dev could see someone sitting alongside it. He squinted a little closer, before catching sight of Grace, ragged, tired, huddled up amongst the roots of her own forgotten kingdom. She clutched Plops under one arm, the broken skull of Cervantes Escobar under the other.

'I tried to fix Plops back up,' she said, watching sparks scatter out from Plops's damaged circuits. 'Robotics isn't

really my thing, but I learnt a thing or two from the other Pioneers before they abandoned our city.'

Dev looked around nervously, as if Esco, Ralto or Sienna might pounce out at him.

'Oh, don't worry about the kids,' Grace said, clutching Plops tighter as if it was the only thing she had left in the world. 'They're waiting for me on the outskirts. Ferns are growing out there now, you know. Sprouts are poking out from the ground. Flember's returning.'

She laughed to herself.

'We're going to find somewhere else to live,' she said. 'We're leaving Prosperity to its new owners.'

'RULE 792, no socks may be worn – FZZZCK – on No Sock Tuesdays.'

'Oh, do be quiet.' Grace donked Plops on the head. She smiled politely at Dev. 'Sorry. It does go on a bit.' She laid Plops carefully on the ground, climbed wearily to her feet, and tugged her haggard robes closer. 'They let me keep Cervantes,' she said, holding the crowned skull out to admire it. 'They removed the mechanics, of course, anything still connected to the city. I mean, he's useless to them, but he's . . .' She eyed Dev suspiciously. 'Well, he's still important to me.'

'B . . . Brianne's *sharing* the city,' Dev offered. 'With everyone. No one's in charge any more. You could come back inside the Spire, if you wanted. Share your own flember with everyone else.'

Grace shivered at the thought of it. 'I had an Oracle telling me what to do, telling me every important decision to make, and I still lost everything.' She shook her head. 'I wouldn't want to live in a city where everyone is considered equal. My flember is *Prime*. It'll always

308

be Prime.'

Dev rolled his eyes and let out a sigh. 'Well, it's up to you if you want to believe that. I just came out here for a walk.'

'Of course, of course.' Grace gestured to him to walk on. As he did, however, he could sense she was still watching him, until finally she called out, 'You noticed it, didn't you?'

'Noticed what?'

Grace's eyes twinkled. 'Of course you did. Of *course*! The heart always pulls us back for a second look.' She stifled a giggle. 'Go ahead. Have your walk.'

Dev stared, confused, for just a few moments more, and then he turned away. He climbed across the power-less cables, the broken glass, the stray bits of smoking armour. Between the smashed remains of the Second Pioneer's fallen statue.

Without the chaos of a race going on around him, however, something about the statue caught Dev's eye. He leant in closer. Rolled one piece of its head towards another. Slowly he started slotting the face back together, and as he did it looked . . . familiar. There was something here Dev had seen before. Something that brought forth strange warm, glowing feelings inside his chest.

'I *know* you,' he whispered under his breath.

He turned back towards Grace. 'The Second Pioneer!' he shouted. 'What was his name?'

'The Oracle told me to keep quiet.' Grace hurried up behind him. 'All the time you were here, she told me not to tell you about the Second Pioneer, as she said it would ruin all my plans if I did. Well, it's not like I have any plans left, is it?'

'Who *was* he?' Dev asked.

'WELL,' Grace announced, 'I told you Prosperity was built by three Pioneers, did I not? And yet only I remained in it – the Second and Third Pioneers both, eventually, walked away.'

She took a deep breath, savouring the moment like a fine tea. 'The Third Pioneer, Iola, I couldn't tell you where she ended up.' She shrugged. 'But the Second Pioneer, I do know. At least, I know what the Oracle told me. It's up to you whether you believe it or not.'

She watched Dev closely for his reaction.

'He went south, he climbed your mountain.'

Dev raised his eyebrows. 'Towards our village? Why would the Second Pioneer come to Eden?'

Dev glanced back to the statue. Its face became more and more familiar in his mind. More and more like someone Dev had seen before.

A thousand times before, right there in his own living room.

In a painting on the back wall.

Standing proudly beside his mother.

While she held a small, angry, baby Santoro in her arms.

'He wanted to go *home*,' Grace whispered.

'It's DAD!' Dev gasped, finally recognizing the cracked face of the statue. 'My *dad* was the Second Pioneer!'

His heart started to pound. His mind started to swim. A million different questions danced upon his lips.

But there was only one answer that mattered.

'My DAD wrote the flember book!'

DEV AND BOJA WILL RETURN
IN FLEMBER BOOK FOUR

Acknowledgements

I owe unending thanks to everyone at DFB, especially Rosie for guiding this ship, and Alison for hammering it together. Thanks also to Emily for your magical skills, and to Jodie, my amazing agent.

And a very special thanks to Sarah. This has been an absolutely absurd year in which to try and write a book, but you've been incredibly positive, patient, and supportive. I'm not sure I could have done it without you.